RIGHT LIVELIHOODS

RIGHT LIVELIHOODS

Three Novellas

RICK MOODY

LITTLE, BROWN AND COMPANY
New York Boston London

Little, Brown and Company
Hachette Book Group USA
237 Park Avenue, New York, NY 10017
Visit our Web site at www.HachetteBookGroupUSA.com

First Edition: June 2007

The characters and events in this book are fictitious. Any similarity to real persons, living or dead, is coincidental and not intended by the author.

Grateful acknowledgment is made to *McSweeney's*, where "The Albertine Notes" first appeared, and to *Year's Best SF 9* (HarperCollins, 2004), where it was reprinted.

The first lines of Emily Dickinson's poem "There's a certain Slant of light" are reprinted by permission of the publishers and the Trustees of Amherst College from *The Poems of Emily Dickinson*, Thomas H. Johnson, ed., Cambridge, Mass.: The Belknap Press of Harvard University Press, copyright © 1951, 1955, 1979, 1983 by the President and Fellows of Harvard College.

Library of Congress Cataloging-in-Publication Data

Moody, Rick.
    Right livelihoods : three novellas / Rick Moody.—1st ed.
       p. cm.
    ISBN 978-0-316-16634-8
    I. Title.
    PS3563.O5537R54 2007
    813'.54 — dc22   2006026937

                    10 9 8 7 6 5 4 3 2 1

                              Q-FF

               Printed in the United States of America

For Amy

Contents

I

The Omega Force

1. The Current National Security Environment

I came to on the loggia—the only question was *whose* loggia? There was the Cavanaghs' loggia, designed by that famous and locally celebrated architect whom I once met. The name is gone. The Cavanaghs' loggia faced the backyard, and they had a splendid garden with unusual varieties of rosebushes. No, this was not the Cavanaghs' loggia. Was it the Hilliards' loggia? I saw theirs when I attended one of the Hilliard cocktail extravaganzas. A hot ticket in these parts. I felt a sublimity at the view of the distant water, the rocky coast, the Hilliards' tulips, ably tended by their one-armed caretaker. No, it wasn't the Cavanaghs' loggia, it wasn't the Hilliards' loggia, and it wasn't the Pritchards' loggia, where my wife once got into a contretemps with the owners of the demesne. Helen (who prefers that I not use her real name in this account) grew red in the face in repelling some uncharitable remark by Sydney Pritchard. We strode proudly toward our *sports coupe*, parked in the gravel turnaround.

I suppose it is possible that I have not visited all the loggias in our municipality, and that adventure was my only purpose in coming to this address, since I had no other purpose that I could recall. Maybe I was keen to see the loggia in question, and that was why I had slept the night through here on the porch furniture of these obliging folks, some rather lovely sturdy stuff painted white and leavened with lime green cushions. However, it's true that in the first light I did not feel particularly well. It must have been a bug of some kind.

The sun rising in the east served as my alarm. As I am fond of saying, I keep the hours of a small child, going to bed before prime-time programming, waking with the light, a light that naturally prompts a fresh bout of reminiscences about the evening previous and its bonhomie. This time of year, early autumn, most of our summer residents have gone home to their suburbs to attend to their law firms or their little boutique money management firms or perhaps to their commercial real estate businesses. The owners of this particular loggia (and the house attached) were therefore not in evidence. Yet their porch furniture remained.

My lips and cheek were swollen from a multitude of mosquitoes that had taken advantage of overnight access. We have twenty varieties of mosquito on our little island, and I think I must have fed every one. Of course, I was wearing my favorite rust-colored poplin shorts and some knee-high socks that went strikingly well with my Docksiders. I also wore the pink polo shirt that my wife says distracts from the blotchy skin problems that beset those of us in the Social Security set. My hair, I'm sure, was badly disarranged. I could barely close my left eye. I hate to disappoint my neighbors and friends by not being turned out in a way that says just who I am: a jaunty former employee of the public sector.

Here's a charming detail. There was a paperback lying beside the chaise longue on which I'd apparently spent the night, a mystery novel of some kind entitled *Omega Force: Code White*, by one Stuart Hawkes-Mitchell. What a baronial nom de plume! The paperback was well thumbed, and no doubt the owners of the house were the consumers of the paperback. Perhaps they had spent some of the dog days just past flipping through the pages of Hawkes-Mitchell's thriller. I decided I should at least have a look, as it was another forty-five minutes or so until I could (a) ask to borrow the commode inside, or (b) make my way along the beach and back toward my own home.

The cover of *Omega Force: Code White* pictured a strapping young man leaping from an amphibious landing vehicle while brandishing a rather alarming handgun, probably a nine millimeter or some such. He was grimacing, this young man, wearing an expression that is to be found in all on-field photographs of football coaches. You'd think football coaches had only two expressions: grimacing and shouting. In the distance of the embossed pictorial image that adorned *Omega Force: Code White*, there was a young woman with an ample bosom. It has not escaped my notice that a paperback cover must always feature an ample bosom. It should go without saying that I prefer antique stories where remarkable people solve crimes and restore law and order using old-fashioned know-how and deductive reasoning. However, I am not one to turn aside a bosom, should it present itself.

Consider the testimonial information on the cover of the paperback. It promised "mind-twisting suspense." I wasn't sure, in my mildly nauseated and headachy condition, that I wanted to be thus contorted. Further, this was the sort of book that would "keep you on the edge of your beach chair." "From alpha to omega, you won't be able to put it down." "The newest episode of *Omega Force* promises and delivers." Who could resist? I was just about to read past the endorsements from the *Orange County Register* and the *Times-Picayune* when I heard a fateful rustling behind me.

It was a French door, and there were drapes on the far side of this threshold (that is, in the interior), some kind of beige drapery, perhaps a linen, a summery weave, suitable for cottage life. And now there was a face in it, a woman's. I caught a glimpse of her at the moment in which she discerned that I was here, reclining on the loggia, facing the beach plums and the massed phragmites, and beyond this overgrowth the sea. Her expression chilled my heart for the rest of the day, as I could not fail to make out the disappointment it displayed. I sat up straight on the chaise longue, like the man of self-respect I believed myself to be, and I prepared some remarks for the lady of the house on the importance of a dip in the north Atlantic on a day such as this. Whatever else the day would bring her, I wanted to assure her, whether feast or famine, nothing would be accomplished through an expression of concern and disappointment. Put a little lift in your step! Whistle a bright melody!

The French door swung open. The woman I've described did not exit the house, did not come to stand upon the loggia with me. Far from it. I could see her chary eyes squinting against the sun.

"Dr. Van Deusen," she said. The chain remained on the door, though as everyone knows, we have effectively deprived the criminal element of any foothold in my town. The criminal element cannot afford the real estate prices, nor can they bother with the tedious ferry ride.

"Ma'am," I said, waiting for her name to come back to me, "it's a beautiful morning, and I was just thinking about a swim. The texture of sea salt and sun on the skin, well, it does *build character.*"

"I'm surprised you can—" There was some kind of sublingual clucking from her, some censorious rhythmical clucking or *tsk*ing, as though I should feel badly about something. And yet so far as I knew there was nothing to regret at all. "Well," she said at last, "can I help you get back to your house?"

I told her that I could very well get back under my own power. Of course, a brisk walk was one of the popular activities in our community of like-minded souls.

"Your wife took the car," she said.

"She—"

"You don't—"

"I remember *perfectly.*"

Memory is an inconsistent retrieval system, as anyone will tell you. It's shot through with imprecisions. Occasionally, things happen that are beyond our ken, beyond our enfeebled understanding. Occasionally, we choose not to linger over events, the way a woman will cast off the particulars of her labor when that labor is completed, when the babe is brought flush into the world. It's this way with me. If I prefer to concentrate on the good things, a lovely bottle of wine, a fine sunset, an afternoon rowing in the harbor in my inflatable raft, who will say that my memory is insufficient? My memory is reliable on the very things it chooses to remember.

"Dr. Van Deusen," the woman began, and again I could hear a hectoring tone creeping into her pleasantries, as when she next said something about the constable. Frankly, I didn't appreciate her point of view. I've spoken with the constable on any number of occasions; for example, about the need for better policing at the ferry dock, about the unfortunate tendency of joyriders to speed down the main road to the country club. I've even advised him to detain certain young people who were frolicking dangerously in their convertibles. I also knew that the constable, whose position was largely honorary, had fiscal problems of his own and would not be drawn into any controversy having to do with this unhappy woman's loggia, nor with my ongoing desire to do reconnaissance on the loggias of my town.

Since I would not be talked down to, there was nothing to do but seize the copy of *Omega Force: Code White* and say farewell to the loggia and its commodious chaise longue. I pulled my polo shirt over my head, briefly getting this shirt caught on my spectacles, and I headed down the winding path to beachside. Did the woman call to me about whether I needed a towel? I believe she did. She asked if I needed a towel, and I believe that I specified that I liked *plush* towels. If there is one thing I cannot stand it is the thin white towel. I called behind me that I would accept a towel as long as it was large, plush, preferably navy blue, and if she could also bring a beverage, that would be welcome, maybe a screwdriver with a twist; I would be grateful for these additional gifts, and if it suited her, she could meet me on the beach, where the waves were rather disappointing for the commencement of autumn, which is, after all, hurricane season. In autumn, you expect some of the finest waves of the year.

Did I overlook to mention what kind of doctor I am? I am a doctor of public policy. I received my doctorate from Georgetown in the early sixties, and in this way it was not required that I serve in a certain Asian police action, though I would gladly have served, because I believe in making sacrifices for noble ideals. There were other impediments that might have made military service impossible, however. I was married, of course, and my wife, who, as I say, prefers that I not use her real name in this account, was in social work and could not be counted on to be a wage earner. Furthermore, our son, Skip, of whom I am enormously fond, had some developmental problems. Skip has spent most of his life living at home with us. So I earned my doctorate, and in the sixties I went on to become an American civil servant. This was my way of *giving back* to the community, working my way up the ranks in the cabinet-level department known as Health, Education and Welfare. It's fair to say that this was not considered a proper job among the men of my family, most of whom went into business. I was good at Latin, I could do a geometry proof like I was born to it, but I was less gifted when it came to reading an earnings statement.

And now what I mean to discuss is the current national security climate.

2. *The Dance of the Stick*

Well, first, let me just add that though I am the last son of an estimable family, one ought not conclude that I am the least of the scions of the Van Deusen mattress fortune. Someone has to be from a mattress family, and so I am, as are my brothers, most of them now passed on to some eternal Van Deusen repose. Though I am the last son and didn't go into the family business, I loved my brothers, and I loved the business. I inherited my share when we sold out to a larger competitor, and this inheritance enabled me and my wife to care properly for our son, Skip, and to live in the style to which we were accustomed. The inheritance also enabled me to retire from my deputy directorate in the cabinet-level agency to which I gave thirty-five years of agreeable service. My wife has had a lot of trouble with her feet in the last few years, but she can still swing a mean forehand when she needs to. She makes her shots.

We have a problem with the beaches on the island, occasionally, and that problem is that when the tide is low in late summer or early autumn, there is a sudden influx of the weedy vegetables of the sea. The day I'm describing was no exception. You could see the effluvia cresting in the anemic waves lapping at the shore. A distant retriever, however, was not deterred from chasing after a bleached stick on South Beach. I was a little uncertain about whether or not I would be plunging in, as I'd foolishly boasted I would to the woman on whose loggia I had just passed a few hours.

However, the retriever reminded me of a pastime that sometimes overcomes me when I am full of the enthusiasms of my dotage. This report will indicate that occasionally I do need to *conduct the entire world*. That is correct. Like most men of taste and discernment, especially those who were born before the ascendance of the idiocy known as popular music, I love the classics, and what I especially like is orchestral music. I love when the winds and the brass soar above the heartrending pathos of the strings. I love the éclat of the percussion section. When I hear such things I cannot but begin to conduct the music, and my phonographic recall is such that in my ears, when the wind is right and the elements are sweet and beguiling, I can *feel* the music, I can feel the 1812 Overture of Tchaikovsky, I can feel "The Battle Hymn of the Republic," I can feel the symphonies of Mahler and Beethoven. Yes, Beethoven. How is it that the music of this deaf syphilitic was so perfectly calibrated to elevate the heart of a tired former civil servant? I do not know. I know only that sometimes I am made to dance the Dance of the Stick, and no stick is better than the parched, whitewashed sticks that wash up on our beaches. On the day in question, I saw the sticks, as in the case of the stick that the aforementioned retriever chased, and I fetched up one of the sticks myself, and immediately I was indicating the accents that began the Tchaikovsky piece mentioned above. I had shed every garment now but my shorts, my socks, and my shoes. I had displaced even my spectacles, I'd tossed them all into the sea, and I had begun my Dance of the Stick as the strings began to swell, and the French troops began to advance on Saint Petersburg, or wherever it was they were advancing. What a day!

Occasionally, I like to *lick* the stick before I begin to use it. It is important to sample its salty surface, just as I imagine the great scribes of the past, the epic poets, needed to lick their quills or their pencil leads before beginning to compose. I lick the stick before I perform, and if the taste does not meet with my favor, I select another, though I do not throw away the first, I set the first aside in preparation for the Dance of the Stick, because it may happen that this first stick is actually the perfect stick, and I do not know yet because I have not taste-tested my new stick against the other. The sticks, on any given day, form a community of sticks, and it is important to understand them as part of a great forest of potential batons for my stick dance. Did Toscanini not select the baton of his craft with equal care? I believe he did. He kept it in a mahogany case. And so, on this morning, I gathered up the rejected sticks, and I stacked them in a sort of a tepee shape, as if I were going to have a bonfire with them, as indeed I might well have done, because if it was necessary that I stay out there on the beach for a few hours, then *survival* might require that I kindle up a roaring good fire to warm myself. I was not yet to that point. I was at the beginning of the stick dance. I was feeling in myself the skewering motion that indicates the entrance of the woodwinds. The happy lives of the Russian serfs are suggested in the passage, but then the skewering motion makes undeniable the gravity of martial conflict, in this initial phase of the stick dance. That is, even though those familiar with the score will recognize my Terpsichore as indicative of an adagio passage, I skipped ahead through some of the pastoral measures, the better to reach the section of the overture in which the cannons begin their fusillade.

South Beach, for those of you who are not familiar with our village, has a former military installation right nearby. The Fort, as this area is popularly termed, now houses members of the community who are in a more entry-level real estate echelon, if you get my meaning, and sometimes people are stuck here for many years, if they don't have the advantages of a mattress fortune to fall back on, so to speak. There are any number of gun emplacements, now empty, facing the open sea, serving to keep tranquil the waters that lead to the major city to our southwest, whose strategic importance will be plain to see. One of the charming features of the Fort, however, is more in the category of adornment than in genuine military relevance, and that is the cannon at the Fort's entrance. That's right, a cannon, from the turn of the century. Ceremonial now, but not to be trifled with nonetheless. I think it is a useful memento mori for young people—who are always engaged in frivolities. The particular relevance is this: I was thinking of the cannon while I was doing the Dance of the Stick, and I began to become rather wild and suggestive in my dance. I was leaping gaily, in my poplin shorts, coming down like a Russian ballet dancer, to indicate that our cannon was firing and that many lives were being lost in this drama of national character. Then I licked the stick again, and the stick tasted peaty and it tasted serious, and what a delight for me, because it had been far too long since I had performed the stick dance last. Why had I denied myself this great and sensuous pleasure? For even if it was rather unconventional, even if my wife told me not to do these things, I felt giddy and I was beginning to spin, as though I myself were the shock wave moving outward from some cannon blast that scattered cavalry and foot soldiers and medics and little drummer boys and whoever else you might have found on a Russian battlefield. And just as I was reaching the crescendo of the Dance of the Stick, I found myself plunging down toward the shoreline and careening into the water, and, in a rather rude awakening, I found myself, well, swimming, or flailing, or flapping, in the seaweedy waters of the north Atlantic, completely immersed, at least briefly.

The beaches where I live, they are not of the highest quality. Those of you who are used to beaches where the sand is actually sandy, where the beach is an expanse on which you can recline, my humble resort town is not for you. Here the beaches are composed mainly of these perfectly round stones, each the size of a conventional softball, and the sandy part, well, it's just some scarce feet at the water's edge. The sand is mainly the action of the ocean upon these softballs. When a great storm comes up, it can erode most of the actual *sand*, so that there is no comfort at all for the preeners and tanners of the shore, in their skimpy little outfits. No comfortable patch on which to fling yourself in pursuit of the volleyball, no secluded rock inlet in which to have the occasional beach assignation, not at all. Our beaches are rugged, and South Beach is the worst of them. Thus, when I fell sideways into the great Atlantic, mindful of the obvious danger that I might be sucked out to Portugal, or farther south depending on the vicissitudes of the Gulf Stream, it was no doubt because of the rocky shore. I simply lost my footing. The fact that I was not feeling terribly well only added to my distress. My stick was flung from my hands, and a retriever happening upon the scene took up my stick and capered off with it into a thicket, where it chewed the stick to toothpicks. Nevermore would I taste the salty, peaty tip of that blessed baton.

And were it not for the water-safety ministrations of a person who effected my rescue, that might not have been the only thing I lost.

3. *A Once Proud Men*

When my wife and I were selecting this resort location for our vacation summers, we made our decision based on such factors as exclusivity, golf programs, cuisine, like-minded persons, and so forth. Never did we think to inquire about the livelihoods of the surrounding population. Of course, an important part of any resort community is its dependent populations. Though it is true, for reasons that escape me, that I am a well-known local character, I find that I am often in contact with the dependent communities, the various laborers in such areas as electrical wiring, plumbing, roofing, plastering, and lawn mowing. I find that I enjoy bantering with these persons, and they recognize that I am not a man of wrath but a man of love. I have only two settings on my dial. Thoughtfulness and joy.

Chief among the once proud men of our community are the fisherfolk. As you can imagine, here in a marine ecosystem, we ought to have a reliable subculture of fisherfolk, out there each morning hauling in the lobster traps or setting out the nets. However, because of poaching from the Nutmeg State, whose marine professionals are a lower class of people, our fisherfolk have found that they just cannot compete, and now many of them have gone on to other sorts of labor. What I am really pleased to report is that some of them have made the move into espionage. This is certainly an area where they can do a lot of good for all of us who are concerned about the national security picture, and, no doubt, they will still have a little time left to set a few lobster traps in the secluded inlets, just so that we'll have something to eat on the big three-day weekends.

How do I know that the once proud men of our community are now embarked on this noble calling of espionage? Well, because of the gentleman who rescued me from the chilly north Atlantic on the morning in question. Let's say his name is Ed Thorne, though this is not his name at all. I would be unlikely to give his genuine name in a report such as this, because it is a federal offense to give away the identity of an intelligence agent, and I would not want to appear frivolous in such matters. In any event, once the gentleman had successfully made sure that I was not in danger of drowning nor of choking on my own spittle, Ed Thorne, who was wearing the traditional hip waders of the surf-casting expert, sat with me for a moment and put aside his state-of-the-art fishing pole, which made my conducting baton look a little silly by comparison.

"Dr. Van Deusen," he observed, "a little early for you to be out dressed like that, isn't it?"

Indeed, I was trembling. Having been plucked from a watery grave by a fisher of men, I found that my hands were trembling as if I had some terrible neurological scourge, and I made an effort to conceal this from Ed by clutching my hands to myself. It's possible that Ed thought nothing of my comportment. And yet in order to ensure that his attention was elsewhere, I noted that it was a marvelous morning, and I was pleased to be out frolicking in it, and late September was the most extraordinary time to be here on our island.

See the gentle reds and yellows on the chokecherry and the ailanthus! See the birds on their migratory overflights! With my distended liver and some of the health hazards associated with that lamentable condition, I told Ed, I needed to take the pleasures remaining to me where I could find them. Ed was rather skeptical about my self-diagnoses, I suppose, but was not one to take issue with a man who has clearly made up his mind. We sat quietly, in the fraternity of early-morning risers. And our quiet was especially natural once Ed made clear that he had heard that my wife was involved in a prolonged house-to-house search for my whereabouts. He also let me know that he would be perfectly willing to help, by driving me to a secure location.

I was seized with a sentimentality about my wife. I did not understand why certain things kept happening to me and why I could not have a more stable home, in which I woke mornings and went to an office somewhere in the house, an office kitted out with the latest ergonomically designed office chair and a fax machine and some other devices with light-up dials, an office where I could work on my memoir about my years as a civil servant or perhaps a treatise on hybridizing chrysanthemums. I was appalling. The once proud men of my town seemed to have a lot more sense than I did. However, it was also possible that Ed was beginning to communicate with me *in code*. It's important to be on the alert for the possibility of code. Listen carefully. Ed was gathering himself up; Ed was about to return to the activity for which he was noted, namely the entrapment of fish, but before he did so, he took pause, and this is when he said those immortal words, "You know, I saw something on the strange side yesterday."

"What was that?" A steady stream of mucus cascaded from my nose, a stream I was powerless to bring to a halt, except with the occasional swipe from the back of my exposed wrist.

"Well, I was just a couple hundred yards from here, down the beach, and the fish were not exactly biting."

By this, of course, he meant that he was near to the airstrip. Because alongside the former military outpost on our island is a tiny airstrip, just a pair of crisscrossed runways, really. They form a kind of an X on the western end of the island, and when the barons and viscounts of our community are in the mood to charter flights, you might see a Piper, Cessna, or even a small jet land here. A faded wind sock, in orange, flops lazily on a flagpole at one end of the tarmac, and there are two or three prop planes parked, awaiting their inconstant custodians. There's no air traffic controller here. In fact, the upper floor of the one remaining structure beside the airstrip has lately been given over to one of the local contractors. That is, even if there *were* air traffic controllers, they would not have a place in which to set up their equipment. Ours is just a modest airstrip, and people drive their cars across it every day on the way to the lighthouse at the end of the island, and let me tell you how they do it: they look up. If they see aircraft, they wait. If not, they drive on.

"I'm minding my own business, the way I do," Ed continued, "down there by the end of the runway"—the runway that, because of prevailing winds, is the less often used of the two—"and I watched a plane park at the end of the tarmac."

"Why, Ed," I said, "that's not very unusual. Don't planes land there every day?"

"Right, except that they don't park so far away from the main parking lot. And then there's what happened *after* these guys parked. That was the part that got me thinking a little bit. These persons, they got out of the plane, and they took their time getting out, and then they were standing around outside. Kind of looking around."

It is true, for those of you who are unaware of the status quo here, that there is virtually no way to visit our island if you are not *already here*. Nor is there anywhere to stay were you to surmount the first hurdle. Were you kidnapped by evildoers and chloroformed and brought here to the island, to be released into the wild, you would find that there was neither inn nor motel to take you in, to give you succor, to offer you starchy towels. So, as Ed suggested, the very appearance here of *strangers* was worthy of note.

"And these persons, I don't know how else to talk about them, except to say that they were *dark-complected* persons. They were dark-complected, and they were standing around outside of the plane, and here's the really unusual part, they had some kind of camera, and the camera had a big lens, and they were photographing the area around the landing strip. There was a lot of photographing going on, all the way around where they had landed. I was sort of minding my own business, but I couldn't help thinking that there was something downright *disturbing* about it, Dr. Van Deusen. I watched them taking pictures, it must have been ten minutes or so, and then just as quickly as they touched down, they got into their plane and took off."

As if the tension were too much for him, Ed once again took up his fishing pole and waded out beyond the edge of the shore, one of the once proud fisherfolk of our area attempting to forge a living from a dwindling fish stock. I was given to understand, astoundingly, that the conversation was now at a close, taciturnity ever being a characteristic of the traditional angler. However, the devastating implications of Ed's remarks stayed with me long after.

For example: though it was true that there was nowhere for the visitor to our island to stay, there existed simultaneously a powerful allure to our enclave. Who would not care to see the affluent and well-connected families of the oligarchy at play, who would not care to observe us up close? Who would not wish to banter or shoot the breeze with oligarchs in the context of luxuriant cocktail party soirées? I know that for many people social events of this kind are not to their tastes. And yet when you have flair and style, you *know* that any party is not memorable until *you* throw your car keys to the valet and stroll onto the patio. Yes, when my wife and I arrive, when we administer our air kisses and firm handshakes, then it is widely known that an island party has begun to lift off.

Now, because of the powerful allure of our island, as I have described it, you will find that curious persons occasionally take the ferryboat over just to see the place for a few hours. Often they bring bicycles, until they are told that the island is largely off-limits to bicyclists, the majority of the roads being under the control of the several exclusive country clubs. Just when the cyclists, with their unbecoming fanny packs, have given up hope, then the pleasure boaters begin to assault our shores with their shameful powerboats or, even worse, those *things*, what are they called? Those things that look like large-scale electric shavers of some kind, inevitably piloted by young men with revealing bathing trunks. These so-called pleasure crafts assault our beaches and shores, and their helmsmen bring tape players and play horrible music, and they roast salmonella-infected meats over open fires.

It was possible, of course, that the plane Ed described carried the sort of *dark-complexioned*, or *dark-complected*, persons who were simply curious about the island, a rumored enclave that houses many storied individuals. And yet you know as well as I that there are certain moments in a life when you begin to see the way things really are. You have just been fished from the sea. You see information systems spread out before you. You understand that divergent and equally important systems of thinking and communicating are happening at one and the same time. You understand that there may be a manifest echelon to human events, and this manifest echelon may conceal much more important subliminal echelons, and this subliminal content is the region of government operations, where secret budgeting processes take place, where backroom negotiations transpire, where deals are cut, and where prisoners are occasionally forced to listen to popular music that is distasteful to them, or are made to touch the breasts of female interrogation experts. This is the way it must be.

When Ed Thorne said what he said to me about the aircraft, I immediately recognized that *dark-complected*, in this context, had a particular meaning, and the meaning of it was that Ed himself was now in the employ of important national intelligence agencies, though I couldn't be certain which shadowy acronym applied. If those of you in the intelligence community are reading these pages, as I certainly hope you will, you'll no doubt remember from your own surveillance operations that the far end of South Beach is noteworthy for two local sites much celebrated hereabouts. One of the sites is the naval radar facility that is still, to this day, engaged in the business of searching the waters compassed around us for enemy submarines and other unidentified craft. The conjunction of that radar parabola (sweeping around in the distance like a heliotropic lily sped up on some nature program) with the facts described by Ed Thorne was totally overpowering. That's what I'm trying to say. Suddenly, I recognized what I had dim-wittedly forgotten. That we were in a time of national emergency! In a time of war! And the first casualty of this war was superficial meanings. Things no longer meant what they seemed to mean. Words had begun to mean more than they appeared to mean. So it was that the employment of the awkward and hyphenated term *dark-complected* here on our vulnerable and pivotal island suggested to me grave international events, events that had mostly been distant from me personally. And as soon as I understood, I began to run in the direction of the other important local site at the distant end of South Beach, the golf course.

4. A Quick Nine Before Lunch

My pace could best be described as a trot. I was taking care not to trip on any of those rocks of South Beach, and though I cannot claim that my aerobic activity met the federal standards for an hour of physical activity per day, I was still capable of vigor, as I have said. Some days I still move around a little bit with my son, Skip, who even though he is in his early forties likes to throw the plastic disk known as the Frisbee. Skip has noted many interesting rhymes for the word *Frisbee* too: *chickpea, scot-free, ennui, DDT, germ-free, squeegee, TV, whoopee, amputee, off-key, deep-sea*—and my personal favorite, *patisserie.* My surmise is that Skip long ago decided, in his unhurried way, that the Frisbee was an important example of athletic prowess among those dazzling and beautiful preparatory school teens who encircled him occasionally, pointing and jeering, here on the island. That particular crop of teens has all grown up now, of course, and they have their own children, children who are themselves nearly teens, but time does not move nearly so quickly for Skip. He is therefore still attempting to perfect his Frisbee skills, in the hopes that those acquaintances of his past will shower him with esteem. It is in these touching moments that I am likely to clap an arm around my son and wipe a food smudge from his cheek. Then I will explain to him that there has *never* been a thrower of the Frisbee who has exceeded him in dexterity and prowess, and this will satisfy his need for fatherly approval, until he hears the hoarse cry of the northeastern blue jay, a bird he much admires.

My objective was the golf course, where I would begin the process of disseminating the information that Ed Thorne had just passed along to me. No doubt Ed was now awaiting some kind of amphibious vehicle so that he could debrief the authorities on the *dark-complected* persons, the current ramping-up of antiterrorist activities along the eastern seaboard, and so forth.

I'm not going to lie and claim that I'm a successful golfer. Just the opposite is the case. I am left-handed, like many creative thinkers, and when I was a young man growing up in northern Westchester County, I attempted to learn to golf right-handed. It was very difficult in those dark ages, you see, to get golf clubs for lefties. My golfing was execrable; my backswing was not to be trusted, and my friends and relations were occasionally injured. In fact, I had bad hand-eye coordination. I did not then (and do not now) let these limitations hinder me, because in my view golf is a fine social activity. As long as you can keep yourself from cursing and throwing your clubs, which I am able to do three out of four times, then you might as well get out there and walk around, even if this only involves disembarking from the cart, fishing out the relevant driver, and limping out to the ball.

To reiterate: my plan was to take my message of imminent peril into the community. It is true that I was, at the moment, a man wearing only red poplin shorts, beige socks, and the shoe popularly known as the Docksider. Moreover, I was legally blind, or at least extremely nearsighted, without my spectacles. I had lost my wallet and all my house keys, and I was soaked through. I had, however, managed to hang on to my ocean-spattered copy of *Omega Force: Code White* by Stuart Hawkes-Mitchell. My style of dress should not have made it impossible for me to carry my message to my townsfolk. I would begin at the golf clubhouse. Accordingly, I crossed the beach parking lot, a mere bald patch, and from there I hiked along the road.

There was an immediate hindrance to my progress, and that was that I espied my wife's car, her little *sports coupe*, parked in the lot by the clubhouse. It is not that I viewed my wife as an adversary, of course. My wife is my ally and my best friend, except when she misplaces items that properly belong to me, or purposefully removes items from the house under the misapprehension that this will in some way keep me from practicing bad habits or pursuing lifestyle choices that she considers unhealthful. Were she fully informed, she would not take these drastic steps.

After all, I am a man who has made health issues an important part of his professional life. Did I not report directly to Secretary of the Department of Health, Education and Welfare Caspar W. Weinberger during the presidential administrations of Richard M. Nixon and Gerald R. Ford? Did I not admire the hairstylings of Secretary Weinberger, the way his erotic forelock curl was swept back and tamed with some old-world fixative? I most certainly did! Moreover, I authored a report on the termination of smallpox vaccination among American Indians in 1974, reasoning that the risk of smallpox infection was so small that it was no longer cost-effective for the department to spend its budgetary monies in this way! I spent three years preparing that report! I know enough about health issues and about my own health and the functioning of my physique to make informed decisions about how to enjoy my retirement years! My God!

The first fairway is the long par four, and it's uneventful, serving as a warm-up for what comes later. Our golf course is a wonder of the world, and many famous golfers have been known to helicopter in to play eighteen holes. The first fairway wants for cover, but if I ran into the one thicket of rough just beyond the sand trap, where the phragmites threatened to overwhelm the fairway, I could easily dash from here to the second hole, which, you'll recall, ambles along the ocean before curling dangerously toward the bluff on which, several hundred yards distant, sits the US Navy radar station, eyes of the world. It would be easy to attach myself to some foursome, the first of the morning, and in this way I could foil my wife, who would not wait long in the clubhouse. My wife hates golf.

When I saw Ned Roberts improving his lie in the middle of the second fairway, I strolled up as though I had just run into him at the village market, where it often takes me so long to produce my change that Ned ribs me about it.

"Jamie," he said, using the diminutive that I have never quite managed to avoid, though I am well nigh upon my elderly years and most of my family is deceased. "What the hell is wrong with your lip?"

"Insect venom, Ned. I'm just out for a little bit of a stroll."

"But you—"

"I really couldn't. I played the other day, and for once in my life I was unbeatable. Let me go on believing I'm a success for a few more days—"

"What I meant was—"

"Well, if you insist, I could take a whack at one or two."

At the same moment, Ned Jr. was attempting a chip shot from the lip of the green, and it seemed to me that the second green was some distant paradise where only the most fortunate of island residents would be permitted to tarry. I watched Neddie's backswing. Ned Jr. had gone into his father's money-management enterprise and was in the process of making a bundle. I'm sure the budding groves of the island, if you get my meaning, were open to him, and indeed his test swing was a marvel, likewise his backswing, and the ball arced away from us, and we could not see its trajectory, though we could see him subsequently pound the air and hop with joy, and in the consideration of this moment, my own heart seemed to thunder with some tachyarrythmia, and my knees buckled, and I was about to go down. Ned the elder caught me by the arm, swearing briefly, dropping his club, ruining his improved lie.

"Jesus, Jamie," he said.

"It's nothing, Ned. Nothing at all. I ate something that didn't quite agree with me."

Ned helped me to the cart, and that was the best he could do in the midst of his intergenerational competition. Of course, a pause in the action suited my purposes because it offered me time to collect myself. I became the watcher of sunlight on the water. What can be more beautiful than this melancholy dream of the late summer? When you have lost your spectacles, and the sunlight resembles the pointillist dabs of an Impressionist canvas. In such a moment, the sun is the animator of all that is, of all that could be. It presides over even global politics and religious conflicts.

Waiting in the cart, I had ample opportunity to return my attention to *Omega Force: Code White* by Stuart Hawkes-Mitchell. Let me note in passing that the current fad for the dangling participle in contemporary literature is more than I can take. Hawkes-Mitchell is not on my side. Also, it's "different from," not "different than," Stuart. And "between you and me," not "between you and I," you cretin. Hawkes-Mitchell, I felt, really needed to open his style manual. Of course, it was obvious whenever the editor swooped in to attempt to make Stuart sound like he had a brain in his head. These were the lucid portions of the text. The passages Stuart wrote himself are the ones in which the detective narrator, Ernest Piccolo, unburdens himself at great length about *beer*. There are also "humorous" references to his manhood, which he calls by names like "Willie the Conqueror" and "President Johnson." These asides are meant to be earthy, but I don't find them amusing in the least. For comic entertainment, I prefer sketches, dancing girls, ribald verse, that sort of thing. Well, enough said on the subject of stylistic poverty, and on the subject of Detective Ernest Piccolo's skirt chasing. (When Piccolo meets the infectious-diseases researcher and refers to the engorgement of his "stalk," the work certainly strains for credulity, likewise thirty lines later, when her "firm breasts belled out into his callused hands." He's known her only fifteen minutes!)

I was able to muster these analytical perceptions on the front nine despite having been deprived of my corrective lenses earlier in my ordeal. This difficulty was not insurmountable if I held the book at arm's length. I could get the gist, and what more than the gist did I require? What was beyond all dispute was the fact that *Omega Force: Code White* had eerie national security ramifications, especially with respect to matters discussed between myself and federal agent Ed Thorne. I would now like to enumerate for the reader the material contained in *Omega Force: Code White* that impacted on these ongoing researches.

1) On page 78, Stuart Hawkes-Mitchell, who cleverly creates a so-called front story, a serial-killing spree, to propel his "thriller," first mentions the proximity of his setting (a resort town on the North Fork of Long Island) to Plum Island, better known to federal government employees as the Plum Island Animal

Disease Center, or PIADC, an animal facility also containing the FADDL, or the Foreign Animal Disease Diagnostic Lab, these two together being designated as a level-four bioresearch facility, right here in our Long Island Sound neighborhood.

2) On page 113, Stuart Hawkes-Mitchell alludes to the possibility that the serial killing is no more than a by-product or cover-up tangential to some kind of amphibious assault on Plum Island (and with it the PIADC and FADDL) by foreign hostiles, which conspiracy according to the infectious-diseases researcher with the bell-shaped breasts was generally referred to as an *Omega Force* among counterterrorist experts, which is the very sort of expert the infectious-diseases researcher turns out to be, an *undercover* counterterrorism expert.

3) On page 249, the Omega Force prompts a so-called Code White, in which military specialists from around the country descend on the coasts of Long Island and Connecticut in an effort to defeat wide release of an airborne zoonotic disease, such as West Nile, hantavirus, Ebola, or Rift Valley fever.

I don't want to give away the ending of *Omega Force: Code White*, because it's possible that some of you in the national military-industrial complex will have the time or inclination to read Stuart Hawkes-Mitchell's fiction. (You may want to skim.) But I don't think it ruins anything to let you know that Detective Ernest Piccolo, who later in the book actually pulls out a man's intestines through a gunshot wound and makes his victim look at them, proved so popular among readers that he was brought back (raised from the dead, as it were) in a number of Omega Force prequels and sequels.

What is important is the presence in this potboiler of Plum Island itself, which is very nearly adjacent to our own island. It's likely that the military has already thought through these issues, that Plum Island is a legitimate military target, one that is well-known to hostiles around the globe, but I would feel remiss if I did not expatiate at length on the issue of targeting, in these remarks.

Before I do so, however, I should add that Ned Roberts Jr. was very kind about driving me around for the next few holes. His father had to ride in the back with the clubs, and this was not ideal, but young Neddie was only too polite, claiming, on the fourth green, to remember taking swimming lessons at the club with Skip, back when they were both young. I watched Ned very nearly sink a hole in one on the fifth, and I experienced only a momentary regret that after Skip's birth, my wife and I were never again able to conceive.

5. High-Value Targets in the Region

We were on the seventh, a long par four. Not much of a water hazard, although lefties such as myself are in danger when shanking. They are going to lose a ball or two. I said as much to Ned the elder, although he's a traditional righty. He was appropriately grateful for my advice, because of his son's three-stroke advantage. I was, however, getting a headache from trying to read the Hawkes-Mitchell, and I was within walking distance of the clubhouse. I could easily have disembarked at any point in order to have a bit of lunch (or late breakfast) while talking over the issues I'm describing here with any persons I might encounter inside. Of course, I was highly regarded at the clubhouse, so that when I turned up there was often merriment among the staff and other members. Furthermore, I could "charge" my lunch without having to produce identification or a credit card of any kind, as I had mislaid my personal identification.

Now, there were any number of ideal targets within ten or twenty miles of myself, the author of these remarks, for those *dark-complected* persons who wished to strike out against our great nation, and some of them are as follows:

A) *Osprey Nuclear Power Facility* of Niantic, CT. The plant has had safety issues in the past, including using seawater as coolant for its fuel rods, though seawater is known to be highly corrosive. The plant has received several citations from the Atomic Energy Commission, which I happen to know—from my own government days—is unusual, since the AEC's initial purpose was, historically, the promotion—not the regulation—of atomic energy. Osprey is good about sending those of us here in the area yearly pamphlets on living downwind of the plant: "What is radiation? Radiation is energy given off in the form of waves and particles. The term 'radiation' is broad and includes ordinary sunlight and radio waves." As it happens, I look directly at Osprey from my breakfast nook, which we added to the house a couple of years ago. My wife was bent on using the very fashionable "modern" architect I mentioned at the outset of these pages, but I insisted that we use someone who was more traditional and able to work in the shingle style for which our island is justifiably famous. The steam rises from the Osprey containment vessels each morning. It's especially lovely in winter.

B) *General Dynamics Corporation, Electric Boat Division,* New London, CT. Few of us here could fail to have noted that snipers have recently been positioned among sandbags at the Electric Boat dry dock, where Polaris nuclear submarines were once manufactured and may be again in the future—if a political office-holder deems it politically useful. Nuclear submarines are the crown jewels of our naval fleet. Many such submarines are moored upstream in the Thames River. I once traveled to see the christening of one, and I was greatly moved to observe the former military men whose recollections of service brought tears to their eyes at the beholding of that warrior vessel (arrayed with festive bunting).

C) *Plum Island Animal Disease Center,* Plum Island, NY. It's only six or seven miles away. There has been, according to the press, simmering resentment between the federal workers on location and the workers from the private sector, who have inferior benefits, longer shifts, et cetera. One way to infiltrate the PIADC and its companion laboratories would be to win over the disgruntled employees, inducing them to commit sabotage as part of *jihad*. Ferryboats leave for Plum every day from Long Island and Connecticut. Ample opportunities for infiltration exist through these and other routes.

These constitute the more obvious targets in the region, though I've failed to mention Shoreham Nuclear Power Plant, Sikorsky Aircraft, the many bridges in the state of Connecticut that are important parts of our national highway infrastructure. And what of the port of New London itself? A nuclear warhead could easily be loaded onto a transport container, concealed as a shipment of sneakers. If major airports were no longer feasible for the *dark-complected* hostiles, what about a neglected seaport town or a tiny little airport on an island such as our island, a tiny little airstrip that is overseen, if at all, only by once proud fisherfolk surf casting each day for striped bass?

I tipped my hat to the Robertses, *père et fils*, though I don't wear hats. I felt refreshed as a result of my time reposing in the golf cart, but now I required an early lunch to fortify myself. Perhaps some lobster salad. As I trod along, I heard a few golf balls whizzing by, like little asteroids in the great unknown of this apocalyptic present. I paid them no mind, nor did I attend to the cries of those who would have me take the long way around. Within ten minutes or so, I was making my way up the steps onto the veranda of the golf clubhouse.

The maître d', Brittany, wife of the fellow who looks after the golf greens, came over to tell me how *terrific* I was going to look in one of the new cardigan sweaters the club was hawking this summer, robin's-egg blue with a facsimile of the island on the left breast. The squiggle of our island, I have recently come to realize, almost exactly resembles the shape of a certain pathogen studied at the aforementioned

PIADC, namely *Borrelia burgdorferi*, which turned up first in a local man just miles from the Old Saybrook PIADC ferry terminal. Where did he contract *Borrelia burgdorferi*, if not from the PIADC ecosystem.

It was incredibly generous of Brittany to offer me this cardigan sweater and even to volunteer to find me a pair of matching golf slacks. Yet I take a dim view of excessive matching of colors, so I was fine with my poplin shorts, even if they looked a little worse for wear. I would accept the sweater only because it was coming on sweater weather.

Soon the German exchange girl came by, the girl who would, she told me in a charming accent, be my server today. I must say that no German exchange girl in the annals of humankind ever looked as stunning as this fräulein. She had steel blue eyes that were almost lacerating they were so vulnerable, and it seemed to me that she had been crying recently. Perhaps the fräulein cried because she knew that there was nothing this life promised that it delivered, which is to say that every human interaction was mediated by the grim facts surrounding us—hemorrhagic fever, Arabs slaughtering Africans, Hindus slaughtering Muslims, Israelis slaughtering Palestinians, and vice versa; children perishing of diarrhea or malaria, dozens of them since I'd sat down for my lobster salad; massive earthquakes; tsunamis that swept hundreds of thousands out to sea; and worse. When you thought of it, if you happened to be a German exchange fräulein working the bar, the world was composed of heartless nonsense, and it was plain to see that all we wanted, this girl and I, was to speak of the necessity for *warmth*, to speak of how irrefutable human kindness could be if it were only practiced more regularly. Why didn't I tell Brittany, the maître d', that the rosy hue of her cheeks could make any child smile, and how lucky her husband was to press his face against hers? Why didn't I congratulate Ned Roberts on the fact that he'd once routinely held Ned Jr. in his arms, that he had whispered to Ned Jr. that everything would be *all right*, even though this was erroneous. How was it that I detested anyone who supported the proposal for a bike path running to the far end of the island? Where was the warmth? When I asked Olga or Nina or Elsa, or whatever her name was, for my Bloody Mary, there was a look on her face of benediction, as if she alone could deliver me from the desperation of my situation, and so I waited with great excitement for her return, and when she brought me the beverage, I told her my secret member number, after which I knew, without hesitation, that it was safe to tell her my story.

European citizens are more informed than we are in matters of international relations. Olga or Elsa listened with cocked head and one perfectly shaved leg bent slightly at the knee as I spun out a web of intrigue. Occasionally, she would brush back some of the delightful hair that fell into her eyes, almost as if these rogue locks knew that their indiscipline made her ever more vulnerable. She was all ears as I explained to her that federal agents were now present on the island, that they were conducting informational sweeps even as we spoke. And because she was so receptive, I then posed first to her some of the questions I now pose here. How did *dark-complected* hostiles discover that our island was an effective launching pad for their plot to overcome our nation through terror? How was it that they first realized the value of this place, this sleepy outcropping in the middle of the Sound of which no one knew a thing, except perhaps the three thousand people who have been coming here for generations, interbreeding, trying to keep out the uncivilized hordes beyond? How did *this* become the high-value target? This was not a place that anyone would bother to blow up with their impressive homemade fertilizer bombs or their dirty radiation-spewing devices! This was not a place that you would release a pathogen! We don't even have deer! That nonsense about a deer washing up on one of the beaches! Have you ever run over a deer in your speedboat? I have been on any number of powerboats that ran over lobster traps! But neither myself nor anyone ferrying me anywhere, in thirty years, has ever accidentally run over a deer's head, nor collided with the broad hindquarters of a buck whose ten points rose above the surface of the Sound like an antediluvian antenna! I have never seen such a thing, Olga, dearest!

Admittedly, I kept her going back and forth, in order to ensure that Olga or Elsa would forever orbit near, and she was thus engaged in fetching me one of several Bloody Marys when the worst of all eventualities came to pass, namely the sudden unavoidable appearance of my beloved wife, my plighted troth, whose search party had now returned to the golf club. There were some raised voices at this point. I clung desperately to the table. But soon I was obliged to cut short my luncheon.

6. Hospital Preparedness in the Event of an
Emergency Featuring High Casualties

The foregoing took place over the course of one Saturday in late September. I mention the day in particular because

weekends in the off-season can be notable for a certain ro-
mance of emptiness. You walk the muddy track of the bird
sanctuary up island, and it's just you and the migratory
flocks. There is the occasional gun burst of the good old
boys with their hunting dogs chasing after the pheasant
with which they stock the local brush. Be sure you're wearing high-visibility gear during these months.

Yet if the weekends are noteworthy for cable-knit sweaters and fires in the fireplace and mulled cider, the middle of
the week is a wasteland, as anyone will tell you. The contractors hasten to and fro in their panel trucks, well over the
posted speed limit, on their way to do cut-rate work for
which they overcharge. The unemployable sector of the island plans its evening benders, just the way the aristocracy
does. There's no movie theater, and the two or three stores
that remain open in the winter open and close in the space
of an hour or two. You can easily pass five days without talking to anyone who is not the postmistress or the woman
who sells newspapers out of the coffee shop. They are each
personal friends of mine. Still, after some chat about the
weather or the local gossip, these conversations can inevitably grow repetitious. Why then would I stay? Why would I
remain here on the island when I could just as easily relocate
to a verdant suburb in the Nutmeg State?

A month passed, a month in which it became apparent
that I was now intimately involved with a conspiracy that
threatened not only the island but also the very liberties we
so cherish. By this I mean I was, during an interval of some
days or weeks, forcibly restrained and incarcerated in some
medical facility on the mainland. During this time, I did
have periods in which it is fair to say I had something like

visions. Some of these were patriotic visions, eagles crushing various opponents, plucking out the eyes of snakes, and so forth, and there were also periods when I imagined I heard the muezzin calling for prayer in a strange guttural tongue. Unfortunately, I was forced to take a sedative in order to aid me in this medical convalescence that I didn't believe was justified. Phantom lights. Strangers calling me by my given names. Conversations with the dead.

I had visitors, and while I want to believe that my wife had and has my best interests at heart, I am not always sure that this is the case. It was Skip who convinced me that I should cooperate with the medical experts who were overseeing my affairs. Skip didn't actually say these things, because he is a man of few words, but it was obvious that Skip, who grows uncomfortable with any kind of change, was upset with the idea that I was not coming home with him and my wife, Helen, whose real name is not actually Helen. It was Skip who suffered when we were not taking our daily walks to the park, nor were we visiting the store together, nor were we pausing occasionally over the cartoon channels on our way to the twenty-four-hour cable news networks. Grudgingly, I agreed to partake in the proffered treatment. Or, rather, I woke one morning and found that I was already participating, whether I meant to or not.

It was determined that there were fewer "temptations" on the island, especially in the middle of the week. I was, therefore, returned to my island address. Among my many dispiriting obligations in this period were meetings of a certain kind at the Unitarian Universalist church. The nefarious modernist architect (alluded to earlier) designed this edifice. He managed, in fact, to make our Unitarian Universalist church look startlingly like an enormous gravestone.

My wife drove me to the first such meeting.

Perhaps it is important to describe my beautiful wife of forty-eight years, Helen Morehouse Van Deusen. Helen has bad feet, as I have earlier mentioned, and she is too skinny for her own good, but she dresses like this is a day on which to be elegant, no matter which day it is, and this likely means that she wears too many dark colors for our island, which generally prefers the bright shades favored by depressive grandmothers and preteens. My wife is never without a certain dark red lipstick and she always wears pumps. She does not play golf.

My wife is a reader; she always has her nose stuck in a book, and had I been smarter, I would have asked her if she had ever read *Omega Force: Code White*, by Stuart Hawkes-Mitchell. In this way, I would have gauged her knowledge of the danger that hovered all around us. However, my wife does not often read books such as *Omega Force: Code White*. She is more likely to be found with a novel from the nineteenth century in which a bad husband is traded in for one who rides well and has an annual income (from a dead uncle) of thirty thousand pounds a year. She does not take out books from the island library because the island doesn't stock the sort of fare she prefers. She buys the books from a used-book shack on the mainland, and she lingers over them with a glass of white wine that never seems to be completed, and then she takes her fluffy Pekingese, Winston, and goes for a walk on the lawn. She needs to quit smoking but has not done so yet. She likes to invite young couples for the occasional lunches, and she likes to regale them with tales of artists we have met, none of whom I can remember.

If my wife served as a foreign espionage agent, then she did so unbeknownst to me. If she were a foreign agent, then she was the best-dressed late-middle-aged foreign espionage agent ever in the history of the United States. To my knowledge, she did not know karate chops or kicks, could not garrote a Pakistani fanatic, and would not be willing to drink red sorghum beer or yak butter tea in order to impress local warlords of the Nile River Basin or the Communist Nepalese.

In the car, out in front of the Unitarian Universalist church, my wife said, "James, promise not to bother them with all these *ideas* of yours."

Now, it's possible that the seizures I'd been having *had* ushered in aphasia. If you believe the medical personnel, I did suffer from brain wave anomalies that could spontaneously clear up under certain ascetic conditions. It's also possible that I'd had more serious problems during the inaugural period of my researches than originally known. It's possible that I'd begun to have a rare and mysterious mood disorder, owing to the fact that I felt I *knew* certain things and was prevented from investigating further by the medical establishment. Whichever the cause, I had found for a time that it was no longer important for me to respond when addressed by most people, among these my wife.

"James, you can fool everyone else, but you cannot fool me. Are you going to feel that you have to talk about your crackpot nonsense? I have no objection to your believing whatever you want to believe, but I don't want you making life difficult for me by creating a reputation for yourself as a—"

I did not wish to cause my wife distress. I decided that I would not trouble my family further, and if this meant that I would allow *dark-complected* persons to land an aircraft on our island, from which they would then lift off and air-drop an incendiary device over the Plum Island Animal Disease Center, so that wind-borne pathogens such as the Ebola virus were then widely dispersed, killing tens of thousands in, for example, nearby East Hampton, who was I to interfere? Helen helped me from the car because I was not walking well. It is not unreasonable to suppose that I had fallen victim to Plum Island's most celebrated export, and my joints were swelling, and my dendrites were occluded, and my ability to express myself was fading away into the autumnal night.

The meeting at the Unitarian Universalist church featured three persons. Myself; a one-armed man, none other than the caretaker for the Hilliards; and a history teacher from the local school, who advertised right at the outset that she had no interest in talking about any *higher power*. And she didn't care, she said, if the meetings recommended that she believe in such a *higher power*. This *higher power*, she opined, was a tinkerer and malingerer who had no purpose but to figure out who were the haves and who were the have-nots and to make sure that the have-nots suffered for the rest of their lives. The only way to improve in this program, she said, was to pull yourself up by your damned bootstraps. By way of example, she pointed at the one-armed man. The implication seemed to be that it was time for him to stop feeling sorry for himself because he had only the one arm. It was time for him to experience a little gratitude that he had any arms at all! There were people out there, she told this one-armed man, who had to eat with their *feet*. Have you begun practicing with your feet? she asked the one-armed man, because you should have a plan in place, in case something happens to your other arm. What if you lose that arm too, and you have to eat with your *feet*, and you have to breathe into some computer contraption to make words on a computer screen appear, and then you would be grateful, I bet, that you used to be a one-armed man. You should be grateful, she said to the one-armed man, who as yet had not made even one retort. I mean, look at *him*, she said, and here she began gesturing at me. Anyone around here could tell you, she said, he used to be *someone*. Ask around. He used to work for the federal government, somewhere in the government, but look at him now, and who's to blame for what he did, there's no one to blame but him, and now he can barely walk, and he can barely put a sentence together, so it's a good thing that he has a lot of *money*, because if he didn't have people to look after him, he'd just be in assisted living somewhere, complaining that his retarded son doesn't visit enough. Understand what I'm saying to you? I'm saying to you that you have to be grateful. Look at me. Do you think I waste time worrying about the things I don't have? Do you think I waste time thinking I could have done more with my teaching than teach a bunch of kids on an island where they don't even give a rat's ass for anything they're getting in school? Do you think I waste time thinking about that? No! I'll tell you what I do! I count my blessings! I count my blessings that I'm not like him! All those men I could have ended up with, I'm glad I'm through with them! I'm glad I'm done with all of it!

After she completed this elucidation of the self-help program that had brought us together here, she asked if anyone else had a "burning desire" to speak. The one-armed man and I looked guiltily at each other. Perhaps both of us would have had plenty to say, but now it seemed that a response would only prolong the misery. We sat in an uncomfortable silence for a good three or four minutes. The schoolteacher riffled through sheets of program-approved literature, as if this were going to ensure our continued submission, and then she said, "Why don't we all say the serenity prayer?"

Since the meeting ended thirty-eight minutes early, I had a good long time to sit on an old mossy bench in front of the Unitarian Universalist church. The one-armed man kept me company for a while, and what he told me, when he had a chance to speak without fear of retribution, was that he was thinking of leaving the island. The same people, the same roads, the same two ways of getting to town, the same enmities, the same movement to the seasons, the same waves breaking over the same rocks, the same unforgiving winter. He didn't see what there was in it for him. He didn't mind pruning rosebushes, and the little cottage that the Hilliards had built for him was charming enough, and that architect who designed it sure was a friendly guy, but—

7. *Modernism and Its Links to Contemporary Terror*

The architect! He was the link! That was it! I could scarcely wait for the one-armed man, with his shirtsleeve flapping like a semaphore, to go on his disconsolate way up the block. Why hadn't I thought about it before? While waiting for my wife to return, I was on pins and needles! The missing causal agent, the conspirator sine qua non, the person who almost certainly passed secrets, and who knew what else, to the *dark-complected* hostiles, was now revealed to me. I experience these revelations, you see, as nearly catastrophic in their gravity. My ability to reason as methodically as I do must be considered a blessing from above, perhaps from the *higher power*. Though the schoolteacher at the meeting might argue that a *higher power* had no place in her newfound life as a motivational speaker, I could but conclude that there was indeed intelligent design, benevolent intelligent design, especially in the matter of conspiracy detection.

Fact: Who was the leading architect on the island? I couldn't remember his name, and the more I thought about it, the more this blockage seemed evidence of the fact that I was being drugged by a person or persons who were anxious to keep me from learning the truth about the Omega Force. And yet even without his legal name, it was clear that the leading architect on the island, by virtue of the number of structures lately built, plans submitted to the zoning board, was the modernist architect I have already discussed. His buildings, it goes without saying, were monstrosities that looked more like the gun emplacements and bunkers of the dilapidated military structure on our island than they looked like proper houses. There were always show-offy adornments like round windows, carved wooden eggs hanging from the eaves, newel posts shaped like lighthouses.

Fact: Who, by virtue of his drafting and planning, had best access to the necessary topographical maps and surveys of the island? Certainly, here again, the conclusion is obvious. The modernist architect was the belle of the ball, invited to every party, every luncheon, where he was inevitably cooed over by the women of the island. This despite the fact that there were serious character flaws to the modernist architect. For example, no muscle tone. The modernist architect did not take regular exercise in any of the popular ways. I had never seen him playing tennis. I had never seen him playing golf. I had never seen him during the adult swim hour at the country club pool. I had never even seen him taking a walk. The modernist architect had no wife. And this was perhaps the most damning thing that could be said about him. A wife is the very foundation of a successful moral life. Of course, I have no objection to alternate lifestyles, and I knew a number of highly effective persons during my days in the Nixon and Ford presidential administrations who may or may not have dabbled in alternate lifestyles. They were fine men who went on to excel in the public sector. But there was no place for alternate lifestyles on the island, which exists primarily as a site for the *socialization of the young*.

Fact: The refusal to join one of the country clubs is a judgment of the traditions of the island.

Fact: There is the matter of his own house, which is in the Japanese style, low and squat, with only tiny windows facing the road and large hedges covered over in bittersweet. I was long repelled in my attempts to lay eyes on the structure, until late in one off-season I sneaked onto the property to assess its ugliness and vulgarity. I'm sure he used chopsticks when dining and served paltry vegetarian fare like bean curd and chickpeas.

Fact: All of his designs, or many of them at any rate, featured the architectural form known as the *loggia*. What are these loggias but ways to insist that persons go outside, and once they are outside, are they not susceptible to any airborne virus that should happen by? Such as bovine herpes mammillitis? Or vesicular stomatitis? Or Newcastle disease?

Weren't the loggias attempts to create a vulnerability in island dwellers such that they were helpless in the event of foreign attack?

Fact: The modernist architect (I remember now, he *does* have a name, Gerald F. Laughlin IV) occasionally wore a T-shirt emblazoned with the logo CCCP. Frankly, I find T-shirt wearing dubious among middle-aged persons, but that is neither here nor there. For those of you who have followed me so far, it is without doubt the case that the T-shirt in question signifies allegiance to the former USSR, or Soviet Union, as these are the letters, in the Cyrillic alphabet, for that despotic regime. On several occasions, he was seen wearing this T-shirt on the ferryboat, in full view of impressionable young people. The Soviet Union? They killed millions! Millions of people were starved by the thugs of the Soviet Union, and the modernist architect had the audacity to wear a T-shirt with this acronym emblazoned upon it? The CCCP was experimenting with biological agents to be used against our nation as early as the 1950s. Naturally, it was necessary for us to experiment to keep up, especially in the area of biological agents intended for use against livestock in their country.

I concede that this evidence about the architect was circumstantial and would remain so, unless I was able to procure a photograph or perhaps a video recording of him delivering nautical maps and site plans and so forth to *dark-complected* persons. I had as yet no such material evidence. Furthermore, it would be difficult for me to obtain such things in my present condition, viz., reliant upon either a pair of canes or the dreaded walker, at least until I should recover a little from my seizure disorder.

In the absence of direct evidence, I will confine myself today to a brief overview of modernism in general and its links to, well, if not terror, suspicious political behavior. According to my analysis, the kinds of personalities who would practice modernism, as I'm defining it, would certainly do such dreadful things as tip off *dark-complected* persons to the presence of a biological-weapons laboratory within six miles of the island on which I was dozing (on an outdoor bench) and waiting for my wife. There was that poet, for example, the fascist one; and there was that other poet, the father of so-called modernist poetry, a vicious anti-Semite; there was, as well, the Irish novelist, alcoholic with a schizophrenic daughter; Thomas Mann, definitely a homosexual if not a Communist, and he abandoned his own country during the war; Fyodor Dostoyevsky, certainly opposed to the czar, and thus a Communist. French artists and writers, that's like shooting fish in the proverbial barrel. You have Sartre, certainly a Communist, his wife, certainly a Communist. Anyone who is French is Communist. If they aided the Vichy government, they were Communists, and if they opposed the Vichy government and aided the Resistance, they were Communists too. Anyone from Africa is a Communist, because all postcolonial writing is proto-Communist or pro-Communist or crypto-Communist; any Muslim artistic endeavor, such as the writing of African Americans, if it's in support of the Nation of Islam, might as well be Communist. Anyone who is tenured at any of the Ivy League universities is a Communist, and so forth. I could go on.

Suffice to say, there is a direct linkage between the hallmarks of modernism as I understand them and murderous, barbarian thugs who would do us in because they hate us and our freedoms.

When my wife arrived at the end of the hour, I was feeling a little tired, and I made no attempt to bring her up to speed on the developments of the case. As long as she believed I was incapacitated, there was little danger of her taking note of my political activities.

8. Online Ordering as Part of the Resistance

Because I am a man of dignity with many important activities to pursue and enjoy in my twilight years, I had as yet failed to take advantage of the so-called online lifestyle. The online lifestyle, in my view, the Internet, the Web, however you might call this thing, was just a highfalutin set of Yellow Pages. Mainly, I allowed my wife, Helen, to do any and all Internet surfing, while I watched television and, where necessary, used the phone to upbraid employees and other hangers-on who were not producing results for our family in a timely fashion. Helen would explain to me things she had seen on the Internet, and I'd have a good chuckle. However, once confined to the canes (or the walker), as I was after being restrained by government-employed medical experts, I found that I had more time on my hands. Accordingly, it became important to gain Internet facility on an accelerated schedule. I am not much of a typist, and in the past I used to pay people to type for me. But there was no getting around the fact that I was going to need the vast Internet databases to facilitate my investigation into the Omega Force and its *dark-complected* conspirators.

How I did this, initially, was by ordering any number of common household items through so-called online vendors. In fact, when I got home from the meeting just described, after a short nap, I fetched my son, Skip, who'd been watching the afternoon light on his sneaker, and I invited Skip to come upstairs with me to where my wife kept the extra computer, an old machine with few bells and whistles upon it. I promised Skip that we would select some toy or other for his occasional amusement.

"You do *want* a toy, don't you?"

It was difficult for me to get these words out, as I have explained, by reason of traumatic neurological event, and Skip, since he was not the sharpest of the Van Deusens, though a fine rhymester, was stricken with the recognition that something was not right with his father. I could see that he was overcome with confusion. In fact, Skip began dabbing at his eyes. He had a nervous way of doing this that was often embarrassing to me, though I had long ago resolved never to be embarrassed by my son. He was worried about his father, who was normally so robust. His father could not speak clearly, was not moving easily, and he could not even have a glass of wine with dinner.

"What about a beach ball? Here, look at this one." I pointed out a beach ball that had the whole of the earthly globe printed on it, and I instantly realized that this would make a very fine purchase for my son, Skip, who sometimes did not seem able to discern between various countries. For example, he was unable to locate Myanmar, though this may have been because he'd never really made the transition from Burma. And what about the Congo? It'd been Zaire and now it was the Congo again. I had Skip read my credit card numbers to me, and then I hugged him. At least I could still do that.

After the beach ball there was a set of fire irons, after the set of fire irons there was a baseball glove for Skip, and then a matching baseball glove for me, and then there was some new bedding for the divan in my office, and then there was a new set of beach towels, and then I ordered entire sets of compact disc recordings of various baroque composers, and then I ordered the great books as selected by professors at important national universities, with special attention to Heidegger and other Germans. When my wife, Helen, began to complain about the online ordering, I changed tactics and began ordering jewelry for her. First I ordered jewelry from Native American artisans in the Southwest, because my wife was very fond of the jewelry of that region, and when she began complaining further about having to drive down to the ferry dock to negotiate with the men in the freight office about the excessive room all my packages were taking up there (it was true, they were moving my packages around on pallets), I then began ordering items from Tiffany and other high-end retailers. All of this so that I could get more time here on the Internet to research *germs*.

Here were some of the germs that had begun to attract my attention. Brucellosis. Venezuelan equine encephalitis. African swine fever. Sandfly fever. Dengue fever. Yellow fever. Marburg virus. Foot-and-mouth disease. *Bacillus anthracis*. Rift Valley fever virus, Zagazig 501 strain. Rinderpest. Miscellaneous shellfish toxins, such as MSX. Dutch duck plague. Avian flu. Ebola fever. Hantavirus. Leishmaniasis. Heartwater. Bluetongue. Staphylococcal enterotoxin B. *Serratia marcescens. Bacillus subtilis.* Coxsackie B-5 virus, Louping ill, contagious ecthyma, Nairobi sheep disease, feline cytauxzoonosis.

I scoured the available databases for descriptions of how to weaponize these ailments. Had they hurdled the species barrier? Had some poor government worker been spat upon by an infected cow and then had himself necropsied like the rest of the nameless cows, goats, sheep, and rodents at the various laboratories? I waited for Helen to turn in. Each night, I waited until she cracked the spine of some dusty tome by Thackeray or Dickens, and then I got up, in my nightshirt and nightcap, and began to limp around the premises.

It was a large old house, designed by the firm of McKim, Mead, and White in the 1920s according to the elegant rigors of their style. The porch was well-known as a gem of this sort. Since we were on a grassy knoll above the bay side, the wind whipped up like nowhere else. As I've said, our island is sweet and gentle and full of breathtaking views and lovely residences, but in the off-season the wind does stay *on duty*. You can imagine how this kind of island living used to drive men to distraction. Late at night, I listened to the winds, and I read about germs, about how these germs were being manufactured only six miles from here, despite demurrals from the Department of Agriculture, whose officials I knew well back when I was in the public sector. After all, the Centers for Disease Control had been under our jurisdiction. I knew that with one good explosion, airdropped from the appropriate height, the PIADC would be dust. Then the millions of innocents on the South and North Forks, and here on our own little island, would be hemorrhaging within days.

With Rift Valley fever, you know, the hemorrhaging is through the eye socket. First you have the high fever, and then the hemorrhaging through the eye socket, and the blood clots in the lens, resulting in blindness in most cases. When President Eisenhower first rubber-stamped the initial experiments with Rift Valley fever, he was reported to have found solace in the fact that the bug was incapacitating but not fatal. That was before the Egyptian variant, Zagazig 501. Now it's fatal.

You would be right to ask if I was lonely during these nights. When my wife called for me to come to bed, was I lonely, knowing what I knew? I am pleased to say that I am given to such Yankee optimism about things that I knew we could somehow prevent these dark machineries of death from reaching our shores. With my rather unsteady hands, I moved the cursor across the screen, turning up any online remark no matter how trivial or alarmist. I felt rather buoyed knowing that I could make sure that my wife and son would not develop painful ulcerous blisters on their mouths and hands that would then give way to harmful secondary infections, ultimately condemning them to anguished, quarantined deaths. Nor would they bleed from the eyes.

When I was done looking for leads, I inevitably checked the weather for the region. The fact that we had not had a major, category-five hurricane in some years did not mean that we could not have one now. And it was with a grim satisfaction that I recognized one night that there was a powerful category-four storm working its way up the coast. Having bypassed the Carolinas and Virginia Beach, the storm would likely be upon us within days. Of course, any such storm would serve as convenient cover for *dark-complected* persons.

The Omega Force, according to the reports of elite government counterterrorist Stuart Hawkes-Mitchell, awaited the hurricane, awaited the night, awaited the blizzard, awaited the war that breaks out elsewhere, awaited a major disturbance in the markets, awaited the Super Bowl, awaited the national holiday, awaited the religious festival, awaited the assassination, awaited any movement or weakness. The Omega Force waited for Plum Island to secure itself, waited for Plum Island to batten down its hatches, and then by amphibious assault in the thick of the storm, the Omega Force would come to liberate the island from the Capitalist running dogs. And the first thing it would do: free the animals.

By coincidence, the hurricane in question was called Helen.

I gummed my food. I ate soup and those small custardy yogurts that practically cried out *gerontologist-approved*. Knowing what I knew relegated me to a singular status, in which there was no one to whom I could talk, no one to whom I could turn. My two brothers died alone. The Van Deusens' success in the world was matched only by their mute, solitary suffering in the personal realm. Neither one of them ever asked to see me before he was gone. No heroic measures were performed. These Van Deusens slipped from consciousness so quietly—as in the case of my brother Chalmers, the venture capitalist—that it was almost as if they'd never actually been conscious. Terrence, who inherited the mattress business, was lost in a hunting accident. He was doing what he loved to do, alone in a duck blind, and he simply didn't turn up later in the day, having been struck by a stray bullet. They were gone, I was left, I was provided for, and here I was up in the attic.

I went for a walk before dawn. I think it was Monday. It might have been Thursday. One of my online purchases was a clam hoe. My wife considered this a reasonable therapeutic activity that I might take up in my dotage, looking for clams on the shore, clams that had not already been infected with a deadly shellfish toxin.

I had a rather unusual garb on that morning. I thought it rather jolly. I wore pressed white boxer shorts, slippers (ordered from L.L. Bean of Freeport, ME), and my purple dressing gown, which was a princely robe. It had a bright yellow lining. I thought of waking Skip, who still slept in the adorable fetal curl of a young child. The wind was howling and beckoning to me, and out I went into it, with my cane and my clam hoe.

When I reached the edge of the sea, which even on the bay side was quite rough, I encountered the former lobsterman Ed Thorne. I suppose I had been expecting him. I had no idea when it was going to take place, the transfer of dossiers, what week, what month. But I was prepared. Ed was just where he was supposed to be, wearing foul-weather gear of the sort you might find in a Winslow Homer painting. We exchanged pleasantries. I asked after his family, whom I had always liked. Then I said, "Ed, are you here with information?"

His ominous reply: "I will no longer be known by the name Ed, Dr. Van Deusen."

"Why certainly, Ed," I agreed. I'd expected it would be so much more difficult to speak, but, here on the threshold of revolution and international instability, I found I was feeling rather energized. There had been an influx of adrenal juices in my compromised system. "Tell me what name to use." I faced the coast of the Nutmeg State. The lights twinkled against violent seas.

"My name," Ed said, "is Ernest Piccolo."

"I've heard of you." I didn't bring up the Hawkes-Mitchell book, of course.

"The reason we have brought you here," Ed continued, "is to let you know that there has been another sighting. An aircraft. At the other end of the island. Just two nights ago. An isolated event, according to the NSA, would be considered a transient sighting, in which the hostiles, understanding that the situation was too *hot*, aborted the mission. A second visit presents much more serious parameters, and the situation, naturally, has now been *expressed* up the chain of command. We believe, in fact, that we have a Code White. As you are one of our reliable local informants, Dr. Van Deusen, we will require your services."

"Anything you say, Ed," I replied, "uh, Ernest."

"We charge you with looking into aircraft design. We have ideas about the design of this aircraft, and we have managed to locate the registration numbers, which are as follows: DB-81404. We suggest that you begin looking into the FAA databases. We suggest that you pursue the licensing information, the insurance information, anything you can find about this aircraft in particular."

I was speechless. The brazenness of the perpetrators! Right here in our resort community! To use a nationally registered aircraft, licensed by our own federal licensing authorities.

"Did you make contact with the hostiles?" I asked. "Did they say anything?"

"Contact was made."

"Were they taken into custody?"

Ernest Piccolo's surf-casting rod never once ceased from its pendular motion. The lure belly flopped on the surface of the black, storm-addled sea. He reeled it in. I could see now that he also had a pail beside him, and that a pair of snappers, in a gallon of briny water, fought back against their imprisonment. Piccolo was loath to tell me what he had learned. Government values secrecy above all. And yet had I not proved that I was a willing participant in the struggle for our values and for our community? Had I not managed this, if little else, in my seventy-three years? Piccolo deliberated before going on.

"During the course of the field interview with the hostiles, I asked what they were doing, and they said they were taking pictures. I told them it was a private airfield, and they said this was news to them, that they had been training here for takeoffs and landings for years. They mentioned Yankee Airlines of Groton. I told them not to be coming around again, that they should consider themselves warned from the highest levels."

"Are you able to identify their nationality?"

"They were *dark-complected*, as has already been reported. Time's growing short, Dr. Van Deusen. We don't have the luxury to be going over points that we've already covered."

"Are you certain it was the same men?"

"Rendezvous here this evening with whatever information you locate. We'll have further assignments for you at that juncture."

Dawn was breaking again. I lost myself in its consideration, wondering when the hurricane would come, if the evildoers would come, when exactly, and *why me*, what had

I done to merit the burden that had been so precipitously thrust upon me? Piccolo, departing surreptitiously, left behind his pail. And evidently he was practicing catch and release, for the pail was empty.

In order to preserve my own cover, I spent the next hours attempting to harvest clams.

9. Contemporary Aircraft Design

What a welcome coincidence that my wife had elected to go to the mainland. For some time she'd wanted to locate a *secretaire* for the guest room. Oddly, it became imperative to her that she locate this piece of furniture before the hurricane. Of course, as I have discussed earlier, it is possible that my wife was a hostile agent. It's possible that she knew the island was now a locus of intrigue. It is possible that she'd been intercepting conversations between myself and Ernest Piccolo, that she knew about the Omega Force and its diabolical intentions, and that, though she loved me, she now realized that she had no choice but to leave me to my uncertain fate.

My wife left on the early boat, trusting that I would not get into any of the locked cabinets in the dining room and that I would agree to return to the self-help meeting, which reconvened in the afternoon. Also, with the aid of our trusty domestic staff, I was to look after Skip. The weather was unseasonably warm and moist, and the sky was bleached white, as if it were the pad on which a momentous story was soon to be written.

I got down to work on the question of the aircraft.

As you know, our airstrip, since it was first created by the military, is sturdy enough to withstand the weight of a full transport plane, with its complement of fighting men. Therefore, as I've said, it's possible that an aircraft as large as a jet could land here. A small jet would be more effective at eluding government capture and could ditch at one of the laboratories on Plum Island, scattering contaminated slurries on the breezes. Or it might collide with the nuclear power plant, likewise broadcasting radioactive materials. Helicopters have also been known to land on our airstrip, as when the most successful of the younger set tries to make it into work on Monday mornings.

These aircraft I have mentioned were theoretically feasible for any assault, and this I told Skip as we breakfasted on sugary cereals. "Skip," I remarked, "I don't want you to tell your mother any of what I'm about to tell you." He nodded solemnly because except on those days when he glimpsed the enormity of his disability, the days when he railed at the world and destroyed household items, he was docile and accepting. He liked secrets, or at least the intimations of secrets. "I'm having trouble thinking all of this through," I said. "There are just too many variables in my head. But here's what I suspect. I suspect that the aircraft the hostiles used was not a jet or a helicopter, because it would attract too much attention. We need to think in terms of small single-engine or twin-engine propeller planes. What do you think, Skip? Piper Cub?"

Skip cried out the name of the plane, "Piper Cub!"

Cereal made him energetic.

"What about the Cessna?"

"Piper Cub!"

A single-engine plane can typically fly five hundred to nine hundred miles before refueling. That would greatly increase the number of available targets. Though it did depend, of course, on where the plane was hangared. The great Lindbergh sparked the interest in general aviation of this sort, and it was shortly after his flight, as you no doubt are aware, that William T. Piper purchased the Taylor Aircraft Corporation and received the appropriate licenses to develop its "cub" model. In 1938, the J-3 Piper Cub was introduced, and it became popular immediately. It was the training aircraft of choice in the postwar years. My own father, in fact, "Dutch" Van Deusen, was known to fly one.

"It's a Cessna 414A," I called to Skip, having long ago left behind my Lucky Charms. Who knew how many hours passed before this felicitous conclusion? I found, by querying the FAA Web site, that there was in fact a Cessna twin-engine plane with the registration number DB-81404, and that the owner was located in Massachusetts. But that was not *all* I learned. It was here that the uncanny part of my story caused me to spill a cup of coffee, up in the study, which would annoy Helen no end. I suspect you will have divined the owner of the plane by now, or the registered owner thereof. But I will make manifest my evidence. The registered owner of the aircraft was none other than one S. Hawkes-Mitchell.

How many S. Hawkes-Mitchells could there be? And could this Hawkes-Mitchell be the government agent who wrote the original Omega Force report, which had been leaked to me by the woman on whose loggia I had spent a night one month before? Was Hawkes-Mitchell working for *us* or *them*? Was he a man who merely dreamed up techno-thrillers? Or did his work involve consulting on national security issues, such that the thrillers were almost certain to have encoded military information contained within them? Did *Omega Force: Code White* precede the actual Omega Force, which I now believed was bent upon attacking the coast of the Northeast, such that the Omega Force was an effect of the novel? Or vice versa? Was Hawkes-Mitchell employed by one of the conservative think tanks? Was he associated, in an earlier era, with plots to furnish arms to the Nicaraguan Contras?

I did my best to enunciate when I called the FAA hotline to ask if there was a telephone number listed for the licensee of the Cessna in question. I made clear that there were legal issues involved. The operator asked if I had a head cold.

"I'm in excellent fettle, and while I'm touched by the thought, I don't have time to discuss my health."

She declined to give me the necessary telephone number, but directory information served ably in that regard. There was a feeling of momentousness when at last I was in possession of the telephone number of Stuart Hawkes-Mitchell. I was not sure of protocol with respect to an actual, living author. Should I tell Hawkes-Mitchell that I'd found myself eager to learn how his novel would end, though in truth the ending was hackneyed and predictable? Was it appropriate to tell him that I hadn't found the character terribly sympathetic? And what if he was not the same Hawkes-Mitchell who composed *Omega Force* but was, rather, an assassin who could instantly cause to be distributed to the island a lethal dose of some rain forest venom that would be admixed with my antidepressants and my antiseizure medication, causing my instantaneous death before the eyes of my horrified loved ones?

I could sense that I was being delivered to the center of the mystery. I waited as the bell tolled on the other end of the line. Apparently there was no answering machine, because the ringer kept tolling and tolling long past what is acceptable in this day and age. At last a tired woman grumbled a curt greeting. Her voice sounded as though she'd had cigarettes for breakfast since years before the surgeon general's first report on the hazards of that product, a health campaign I personally helped implement.

I asked for Stuart Hawkes-Mitchell.

"Excuse me?"

I asked again for S. Hawkes-Mitchell. Or Mr. Hawkes-Mitchell.

"I'm inquiring into the whereabouts of Stuart Hawkes-Mitchell."

"Well," she said, sighing mournfully, "I'm sorry to tell you then that Stuart is dead."

"Dead?" As the author might have said himself, I could *scarcely believe what I was hearing.* "But I just read his book, and it was . . . a pretty good book."

"Stuart died last year, I'm afraid."

"Would it be possible to ask how he died?"

"Who's asking?"

I blanked for a moment, trying to come up with an appropriate pseudonym. "Well, this is Ned Roberts Jr. I'm an amateur pilot, looking for a, uh, I'm looking to buy a Cessna Skyhawk or similar model, and I was doing some inquiries into persons in western Massachusetts who might be interested in—"

"We don't have the plane anymore."

"I see, well, I—"

"Stuart had an accident in the plane."

"He—"

"That's right."

"You mean the plane with serial number DB-81404 met with a . . . with a fiery conclusion?"

"I hated the plane right from the beginning, and I told him to get rid of it."

I continued to stress the consonants in my words, such that I probably sounded like a speech professional to her. "And you say this tragedy took place last year?"

"About fourteen months ago."

"So there was no chance that he was . . . because you see I could have sworn I *saw* the plane . . ."

It was then that I began to hear in her voice a growing suspicion. I couldn't help, however, but push my inquiry to its logical conclusion. It was all clear to me now. I could see it as plain as the headlines on tomorrow's daily papers. Stuart Hawkes-Mitchell, by virtue of his imagination, had breathed into life the Omega Force series long before recent global political events. Hawkes-Mitchell was trying to make an honest dollar, though he had in fact dreamed up a rather dreary thriller with unappealing characters. He was naturally unaware that the story had somehow spawned a genuine Omega Force, this cadre staffed entirely by *dark-complected* persons. Naturally, in the course of beginning to use their assault capability just as Hawkes-Mitchell had planned it, it had become necessary for the Omega Force to kill off the author himself, the artificer, lest he reveal the linkage between his pulp novels and the planned assault on the PIADC or the Osprey Nuclear Power Plant.

"I'm sorry," Mrs. Hawkes-Mitchell said. "I'm going to hang up now."

"Wait," I cried. "Just one more question!"

Many points remained to be resolved. Why was our island now central to the Omega Force? Why had I happened to find Hawkes-Mitchell's all-important piece of fiction on the porch of that house, when the Omega Force would have perhaps preferred that I never find the book? And why did the plot, here in the real world, feature woebegone individuals: a modernist architect, a German barmaid, my learning-disabled son, and an out-of-work surf-casting lobsterman?

I had my face in my hands. And I would have stayed that way for a while were it not that I suddenly felt Skip's large, meaty palm on my clavicle.

I looked up into his soulful eyes.

"Shall we go for pizza?"

10. On Beach Parties and International Disarmament

There was only one venue on the island for that popular culinary item known as pizza pie, and that was the bar named Dumpling's. A dangerous location, Dumpling's, and not simply because of the presence there of sodium and trans fats. Sinister characters lurked in the margins of Dumpling's. They nursed lethal intoxicants meant to prove, through ingestion, their ability to survive anything, any degradation or humiliation at the hands of the affluent. I should not have gone into Dumpling's. I was not dressed properly, for one. In any kind of scuffle that would result from our presence, Skip and I were sure to fare poorly. Neither of us was terribly strong, nor were we schooled in the proper sorts of self-defense techniques.

Additionally, my wife had taken the car. And I had given the domestic help the afternoon and evening off. There was no recourse but to walk to Dumpling's, and as we went, I held tight onto the arm of my son to steady myself. I am sure that in Skip's view this amounted to a noble responsibility, being able to guide his old father along in the world. As we walked, we played the rhyming game. That is, I allowed Skip free rein with respect to this peculiarity of his character. I would select a word, like *storm*, and then I would challenge Skip to come up with the greatest number of possible rhymes. *Swarm*, *warm*, *dorm*, and the dazzling *fungiform*. I even allowed Skip to use the ersatz rhyme of *orn*, so naturally he scored heavily with *warn*, *torn*, *scorn*, *mourn*, and, to my horror, *porn*.

I'd left my goodly wife a note explaining where we had gone, so that when she returned on the late boat she might find us, but it was my belief that by the time she reached Dumpling's we would be well on our way to meet Ernest Piccolo.

I was glad to behold the expanse of bottles in Dumpling's. I loved the way these mixables were arrayed, like the tiered dancers on a Busby Berkeley riser. Always in front of a mirror too, so that their tableau would be twice as seductive. I kept as far away from the bar as I could get. I installed my son by the foosball table (I believe this is the name of the game) because he was inordinately fond of foosball, as I had found on a previous visit, *ruse*ball, *brews*ball, *Jews*ball, and I hustled to the bar quickly to lodge our order. I carried back a lamentable seltzer water with lime while we waited for our french fries and other salty preliminaries. I could taste the moment of hypostasis, I could taste the *ousia* of drink, even at this distance from the bar, the way in which all mystery would be made comprehensible. Who knows but that I would have weakened right then and there—as we picked lazily at our french fries and Skip eyed the foosball table lustily—if a staff person in Dumpling's, someone unknown to me, had not begun shouting for no fathomable reason. This crusty publican was outraged about some patron sitting near to us, but I could not identify the offending individual. "You got a lot of nerve coming into this place! Some people got a helluva lot of nerve!" Initially, I feigned ignorance about the disturbance, as did many others. I searched discreetly for the target of the aggression, but in vain. The ripostes only amplified. "All a man like you does is lie around like you couldn't be bothered to—"

Soon there was another fellow with him, an apron-wearer, and they were walking toward the section of the establishment reserved for those of us dining. I believe the apron-wearer was cleaning a knife on a rancid dishcloth. Without further delay, I took hold of my son's hand, and I told him that we needed to change venues immediately. I told him, in a tumble of words, that we needed to hurry now, that there were treasonous elements everywhere around us, enemies of the state, and it was no longer safe to be in Dumpling's, especially in light of the altercation that was almost certain to take place. I told Skip that we would have the pizza delivered, and we could microwave it, and it would taste just as delicious as if we got it right here, fresh from the brick oven.

There was some bushwhacking to do. There were some back roads and some clambering through the boxthorn and blackthorn, until we were again at the water's edge, beholding the drama of the swells. It wasn't so far. The moon was on the rise, despite the storm that was predicted in the marine band forecast. The thick humidity of early autumn was an oracle of summer's undeniable last gasp. Through hurricanes does summer relinquish its grip. With a little more hardship, we would step from the overgrowth behind the house of a certain mergers and acquisitions specialist and into the moonlight. That is, we soon found ourselves on Carson's Bluff, a spot of gentle dunes a mile or so beyond the end of the golf course, and as we overlooked the lip of the land, we could see that the waves had grown unruly and restive. We threaded our way down an eroding path, catching on to dune grasses to avoid plummeting to our deaths below.

In the distance, a robust beach fire flickering. A bona fide beach fire of the sort that the neighbors' kids used to have once or twice a summer, getting into whatever trouble they got into. Of course, I worried that this beach fire not only was unsafe but constituted a security breach in the matter of our objectives. For if one of the beachcombers from the gathering was hiding out in the nearby brush, it would be virtually impossible for me to keep this individual from recognizing that a high-level exchange of information was about to take place. Unless I neutralized him or her. As I was thinking this thought, I was disturbed by another interloper on the scene, perhaps an attack dog! A pit bull or a German shepherd sent to menace us! I distracted the hound by pulling on the stick in its mouth, which prompted it to yank back, growling ominously. I could tell that my technique, disarming it with play, had won over the attacker, because its growls had now given way to a relentlessly wagging rump end.

The stick, of course, was a perfectly shapely and sea-worn example of Atlantic driftwood, the kind of stick that may have been thrown into the sea and fetched out by dogs like this for decades now without ever having been chewed to saliva-moistened bits. Skip and I were trying to persuade the dog to return to its masters, but it was having none of it. Instead, it expected us to cooperate in this ceaseless throwing of the stick. Skip was about to oblige, though he didn't throw very well, but something in me steadied his arm. I took the stick from him. I could feel it overcoming me, that *humiliating need.* Now was *not* the time for the Dance of the Stick, with all that was upon us: an amphibious landing by the Omega Force, intent on commandeering the island for a multipronged assault, a shock-and-awe-style assault on multiple military targets in the environs. The Omega Force was aware, no doubt, of the presence on our island, at least during the months of summer, of a member of the House Armed Services Committee and a deputy director of Homeland Security, likewise numerous members of the party in power. Each forking path of possibility had been duly accounted for by them. There was no time for the stick dance, and yet I felt an inability to sit still or to think clearly. Still, I didn't want Skip to witness me in the middle of what was certainly, at best, an eccentricity and at worst a sign of some nervous disorder that I had never quite eradicated despite years of treatment.

Skip was beginning to shiver.

"Want to wear my jacket?"

Skip shook his head dramatically. I forced the jacket on

him. A man who knew what I knew could not afford to be wrapped up in outerwear. And then I took off my loafers. It was easier to walk in the sand without them. The seconds passed interminably. No fisherman appeared on the shore. Was it true that there was no choice but to make our way over to the beach party? To do reconnaissance in that area? It seemed there was no choice. The attack dog chaperoned us.

Did I recognize those urchins of the neighborhood? Urchins no longer. They were the mostly grown children of privilege. Grown children who had never known a day of being short for change in their lives. They carried no cash. Grown children whose hair was perfect, whether combed or disarranged, from the moment they were expelled from the womb, and who seemed to know, even then, exactly how to ski, exactly how to do that nonsense on the surfboard with the sail on it, whose gift for repartee, even in their twenties, would exceed mine over the whole of my tired life, who would succeed effortlessly in lives that would be noteworthy for an absence of self-reflection despite reversals, illnesses, or death. Their mysteries were so buried that they were inaccessible even to themselves. As the fashions of the years turned, these young people remained unaffected, unperturbed, and by virtue of their lack of interest in the goings-on of the world, as perfectly lovely, as luminously beautiful and purposeless, as the hosts of heaven.

What was unclear, as I gazed around at the group of them, all delinquent from classes at the colleges in the area in preparation for a long weekend, was whether or not they were *collaborators*. Would collaborators be making the camp-fire dessert known, Skip helpfully pointed out, as the *s'more?* Because amid their other nefarious activities, about which

I had as yet not enough information to surmise, there was the preparation of this dessert. It could just as easily have been some explosive preparation, gelignite or TNT, who knows, and maybe these supplies had been secreted away when the scouts had given word of our approach. For the moment it was the *s'more*, prepared in the traditional way with stick, marshmallow, graham cracker, chocolate bar.

I was immediately hailed by name. "Dr. Van Deusen," one of the young men called to me. Did I know him? Whose son was he, and why did he look so much like so many other people? Like sons who had perhaps by now grown up and had sons themselves, in some eternal return of Anglo-Saxon reinheritance. He could have been anyone on the island, and that alone made it impossible to establish his intentions. "Care for a beer, Dr. Van Deusen?"

As any espionage agent will tell you, it's important to be able to blend in with the indigenous cultures, and if this means garroting a one-legged prostitute in Bangkok in an effort to establish that you are not sentimental and are willing to take risks, then you will have to garrote that hussy and pray to God that you will be forgiven. Accordingly, while attempting to fathom the purpose of this so-called beach party, I had no choice but to partake of the local grog and to attempt, at least in brief, to make nice with our hosts.

I introduced Skip, and I was asked if Skip would like a beer too. Though Skip was beginning to go gray early just the way his father had, with a full head of hair that would need to be carefully treated with some masculine dye, we did not permit him to drink alcoholic beverages. It only confused him. I demurred on Skip's behalf, to his disappointment.

From the first sip of the beverage, I realized that these were not such bad kids after all! In fact, maybe they weren't such carbon copies of their stuffy parents as I believed them to be! Maybe there *was* a little something going on in there. A little understanding of the complexities of the world. Perhaps they were able to understand that everything that was so felicitous to them, their way of life, was about *exclusion*, and that this precious exclusion, in which they got to romp on the beach with the same kids with whom they went to their preparatory schools, was something that they needed to *defend* somehow, whether through public service or through the participation in the foreign bureaus of the Central Intelligence Agency or similar organizations.

The youngsters, they now informed me, had been about to undertake a certain drinking pastime. According to this game, one either had to answer a question with a revealing truth about himself or else he had to drink. The youngsters now revealed that there was a rather powerful punch lying in a cooler not far distant, just beyond the merry light of the bonfire, a punch that had some preposterous name such as From Here to Eternity. The drinking game was already under way, and there were already some bodies lying around. Whether in the midst of premarital fornication or unconsciousness was hard to know. Perhaps there had been a ritual poisoning or perhaps powerful sedatives had been stirred into the beverages by malingerers in an effort to sideline various parties in the military battle to come.

More pressing, in a way, was the rule that in certain circumstances the players were required by the drinking game to embrace or even kiss one another. I pointed out to a young blond fellow with a backward baseball cap (and one of those preposterous necklaces) that this was a requirement from which I needed to be exempted, by virtue of advanced years. The towheaded son of the president of one of the country clubs, I believe, whose name was D'Arcy, said that this should elicit *no worries*, because I could always just *drink some more*.

I reluctantly assented. D'Arcy again asked if I didn't want Skip to play.

"He's very sensitive about things like this. And at any rate, he's more interested in rhyming games. He's a demon for rhymes."

A young woman who had been sitting on the far side of one of the enormous logs on the beach appeared from the shadows and demanded, with a sloppy grin on her face, a demonstration of Skip's rhyming skills. Skip sat quietly at my feet, looking out at the ocean, since the sound of waves often pacified him.

"Skip, my boy," I asked, shaking him, "can you give an example for the good people of a rhyme for the word *orange?*" This was a trick question, of course, because there are no perfect English rhymes for *orange*, as Skip had properly observed on many occasions.

"No rhymes," Skip said darkly. "Change, mange, short-range, strange, arrange, derange, estrange, exchange, short-change." And then he got stuck on *mange* for a while and kept whispering it to himself.

A contestant, Meghan was her name, was asked by the moderator for a penetrating truth about herself, and she admitted that she'd cheated on every test in geology, a required course in her core curriculum. This was not considered a penetrating truth, and Meghan laughed gaily as she swigged another dram of From Here to Eternity.

Let me pause briefly to observe that *Omega Force: Code White* by Stuart Hawkes-Mitchell has the requisite stunning reversal in its last chapters, and this I learned by borrowing one of the multiple copies of the book from the shelves of our tiny island library after I had mislaid the earlier, purloined copy. Why would there be multiples of such a book on our island? Let us leave this question aside for the moment. The *stunning reversal* in the Hawkes-Mitchell tome is as follows: Ernest Piccolo, the astringent detective at the heart of the saga, it is revealed, has all along been in cahoots with the Omega Force. That the book shifts abruptly from Piccolo's point of view to the point of view of a small-town lawyer named Bonnie Peebles is one of the few unusual features in what is basically hackwork, and it enables Piccolo's betrayal of Peebles, notwithstanding his claim to have fallen in love with her after a grand total of two romantic evenings; Piccolo waits until they are on the verge of landing on Plum Island in their stolen Coast Guard launch, and then he puts his .38-caliber wheel gun to her head and tells her that since she's the only one who is in possession of the *real story*, she's the one who's going to have to *die*.

Frankly, I couldn't have lived with Piccolo for another fifty pages, and his novelistic urge to spill the entire story in his last speech is difficult to take. Still and all, whichever jihadists brainwashed him had already prepared for this moment, the moment when he enacts the murder of his doomed romantic obsession. Meanwhile, the Omega Force has plan B in place. Either Piccolo murders the small-town lawyer, and the Omega Force reaches the PIADC unimpeded, or he does not. But by distracting Bonnie Peebles, by encouraging local law enforcement to follow the stolen Coast Guard launch, the Omega Force ensures a clean getaway, in scuba gear, so that they can live to fight another day—in the next Stuart Hawkes-Mitchell sequel.

It was the realization that such a stunning reversal—the imminent betrayal by Ernest Piccolo, a.k.a. Ed Thorne—might already have been in the offing that led me to undertake some quiet interrogation of the persons gathered at the party. Sotto voce, naturally. I was performing the role of the intoxicated retiree, and performing, I must say, with a certain spirited aplomb. As soon as I had what information I needed, Skip and I could repair to the brush beyond, to see if men in wet suits were indeed scrabbling up the eroding face of Carson's Bluff, just out of view.

To the contestant named Meghan I mumbled the following question: "Was a rather gruff man called Ernest Piccolo here earlier in the evening? Before we arrived?"

"Who?"

"Ernest Piccolo. Rough-hewn, salty guy, curses like a sailor. Might have attempted to take advantage of you."

"I don't know what you're talking about."

"Excuse me, then. Thank you for your time."

11. Policy Recommendations

To maintain deep cover, it was crucial that I should be seen serving myself more of the punch, so I poured a liberal amount of it into one of the plastic cups available. Just beyond the punch, a strapping young man I recognized as one of the soda jerks from the ice cream establishment in town was singing quietly to himself. He too had liberally sampled the punch, and he was well on his way from here to eternity. I asked him if there had been an infiltration of this beach party by person or persons unknown to him, *dark-complected* persons, persons who might seem to have allegiances to foreign powers, particularly powers of a globalist perspective, powers that were aligned with uncontained growth of a united Europe, or perhaps powers that had a pan-Arabist or pan-African worldview. Did he perhaps see Sudanese Arabs coming down the beach? Riding Arabian stallions, bent on some kind of ethnic cleansing? Did he see any of these things? Anything out of the ordinary? Anything at all?

The soda jerk stopped singing abruptly and fixed me with a rheumy eye. "Damn straight," he said. "Damn straight, I did. I saw them. I saw them all around. There were guns going off. They were running up and down the beach and they were raping and pillaging and they were stealing everything that was left to steal, everything that wasn't screwed down. They were stealing people's television sets, especially the flat-screen ones, and they were stealing the satellite dishes because they knew with the satellite dishes they could make us all watch Arabic-language cable stations, and they were taking the family silver, and they were melting it down and they were making statues out of the silver, fat Buddha, Mohammed, Ganesh. And they were stealing the expensive twenty-speed racing bikes with the little mounting thing where you put the bottled water. Oh yeah, and the cars. They took every Hummer on the island, every one of those Hummers on the island, they took them, and they made some kind of military convoy with all the Hummers. And the tank, the guy who owns that tank and drives it down to get the newspaper, they took that guy's tank, and they actually ran over him with it, because nobody should own a tank, not even as a joke."

The young man did not stop here. He went on to describe a host of signs of the invasion. The hostiles took a lot of clothes because, the young man said, there was nowhere else on earth you could get clothes in these colors, and the clothes would serve as camouflage. They went rampaging into our town, seizing hostages along the way. They stole all the trunks of garments from the Lilly Pulitzer trunk show. And then these *dark-complected guys* broke up some barbecues that were under way, because, the young man told me, the food was too bland, and when the strict Islamic sharia was adopted on the island, whoever hadn't died a nasty, violent death was going to have to learn to mash their own chickpeas, and they weren't going to be able to drink alcoholic beverages, because that was part of the sharia, no more drinking. "And because we knew they were coming," the soda jerk continued, "we came down here, because hell if we're going to watch them pour out all the rest of the booze when we could have the chance to drink some of it ourselves, so we came down here to wait for it all to happen."

These were his words! Raping and pillaging! Arabic-language cable stations! Lilly Pulitzer! Strict Islamic codes! I stared at him for a moment, absolutely uncertain about what I should do. Knowledge itself had been vitiated, vaporized, obliterated, in the international conflict flourishing here on the island. Old-fashioned know-how was the thing that once brought the constellations into focus, the Big Dipper and its neighbors. Knowledge was the thing that enabled you to read the morning paper, to digest the day's events; knowledge was what you used when you were telling your son what to believe and what to ignore. But knowledge and certainty had been wiped out in the conflict at hand. It was now impossible to verify anything at all. I'd had weeks to research and to cross-reference all the various strains of the story. I'd found that an architect on the island was illegally building modern architecture against the wishes of the local citizenry, and through these structures, through the heretical cult of modernism, he was indoctrinating people into decadent lifestyles and signaling about this to Islamist compatriots. I had learned that people with dark complexions had been landing on our island in small aircraft, as witnessed by our once proud fisherfolk, and these people were taking photographs of our island, without permission, in an effort to mount attacks on high-value targets in our neighborhood, where certain rogue elements were also beginning to experiment with increasingly unstable germs.

Which side was which? The sides had become indistinguishable. The government position either included my own wife, who was acting in a way that was frankly conspiratorial by my standards, and Ernest Piccolo, who may or may not have been a once proud fisherman of our island, or who may or may not have been a character in a novel called *Omega Force: Code White*, a novel that may or may not have been written by someone called Stuart Hawkes-Mitchell, whose own Cessna aircraft may or may not have been the one flown to this very island by certain *dark-complected* people, or else this Cessna aircraft may have gone down in a fiery crash in western Massachusetts, which suggested that he was either a casualty of the *dark-complected* or he was a confederate of same. Was Hawkes-Mitchell on the side of the government? Was he attempting to suppress a revolution? Or was he attempting to hasten it? Was the government attempting to control the revolution or not? Was the government for the people or against the people? And on what basis was it possible to ascertain these things?

I shook the young soda jerk roughly in an attempt to get him to answer further questions, but he was now apparently disinclined to respond. In any event, my attention was called away because, sitting on the great white log by the bonfire, the young man called D'Arcy was now offering Skip, my beloved son, heir to all that I had done and would attempt to do, *some of the punch.* Now my son Skip was drinking the punch and I was rushing to my son's side, where unfortunately I had no choice but to slap the cup of punch out of his hand.

"Listen up, all of you young people. Listen up! I have something to say. Listen to me!" I looked at the assembled faces, in various stages of dishevelment. "It's important that you understand what's taking place around you—" And, realizing that this was a rather provocative assertion, I—

"Shut up, Dr. Van Deusen," one of the kids called. "Answer a question or have a drink."

"I will *not* shut up," I said, my pride rising. "Please. Listen for a moment while I make some observations about current events."

Another voice cried out, "Ever spent a sober day in your life? That's *your* question!" Much snickering.

And then suddenly Skip was running off. My son was fleeing the scene. Owing, no doubt, to some tiny slight. I saw his handsome body, his stunningly handsome but empty-headed vessel, disappear into the darkness beyond the bonfire, a darkness that quickly enveloped whatever came its way. I picked up the nearest piece of driftwood that was at hand, and I closed in on the master of ceremonies, young D'Arcy, with intent to batter his person. But then it was there in my hands, the precious stick, and I could feel the stick calling to me. Above were the stars, wheeling in the dispassionate sky, and there was the hypnotic flickering of the fire, and before I had a chance even to think about what was happening, I was led by the stick into the night, following my son. I was hearing the ringing of the symphonies of strategic information, the contemporary symphonies, the symphonies of the *civilian dead*, and I said to myself that this was just absolutely *wrong*, and yet I felt my legs, my toes, my ligaments, my sinews, beginning the dance, the dance of death, on the shore of the beach, just out of the ken of the youngsters, who no doubt had begun to climb into one another's arms. I began to cackle bizarrely. I knew arcane things that were lost to the historical record, and I was dancing and spinning like some Sufi master. I was a beacon on the shore. I was *the sign*, because there was always a sign, there was an indication, a first shot, a lantern in a window. It was clear! It was clear that I was meant to wake on the loggia, it may even have been my *own* loggia. I was meant to see Ed Thorne, double agent, meant to hear his story; these things lined up. The Omega Force knew that I would walk from the house at dawn. They knew, when they saw the Dance of the Stick, that it signaled the end of the West, the end of the American Century, and Ed Thorne told me what he needed to tell me, that they would come, the Omega Force, to set American against American. Ed Thorne was where he was meant to be, and when I heard what he had to say, I embarked on my researches, researches that brought me here, where, of course, I would repeat the Dance of the Stick, I would begin my foul dance, my ghoulish jig, and I would cast off my clothes. There was no other interpretation possible. It was I who was to invite in the Omega Force and its foreign agents. I was powerless to stop them, and in this dream I danced to the death, with the stick whose only wish was to be again in the sea, scrubbed by salts and storm tossed, and I would not bend to its will, and so we fought, the stick and I, a pitched battle, and the stick wrested me to its purpose, to be adrift, yes, as the great poets have always known, *dulce et decorum est pro patria mori*, it *is* sweet and fitting to die for your country.

II
K&K

Ellie Knight-Cameron oversaw the suggestion box at Kolodny & Kolodny, a small insurance brokerage company, and in all the many years of discharging this humble task, she'd never come across a suggestion like the one she discovered Monday nestled in that cardboard container: *If they're going to close lanes on the parkway, they ought to actually repair the goddamned road.*

K&K, as they abbreviated themselves, were located in the sprawling suburban municipality of Stamford, CT, a mile or so off the High Ridge Road exit of the Merritt Parkway, and for some years now this verdant stretch of pavement had been a maze of lane closures, especially west of town. The majority of K&K's ten employees commuted into town *against* the prevailing traffic, and it was here that they often encountered the dreaded file of orange cones.

Without a doubt, this suggestion she found was reasonable. Excepting the split infinitive and the profane language. People complained about traffic. It was one of the things they talked about. Still, it was hard for Ellie Knight-Cameron to imagine what she, as office manager, was supposed to do about it.

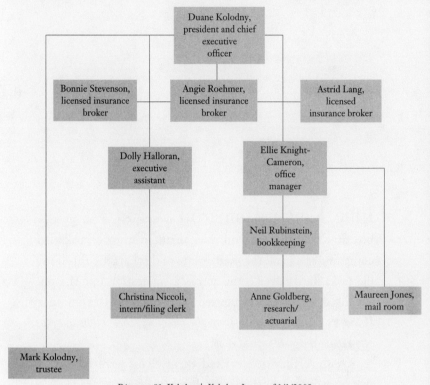

Diagram #1, Kolodny & Kolodny, Inc., as of 1/1/2005

Ellie had nothing much in the way of organizational power. In fact, the suggestion box existed mainly to enforce camaraderie at the K&K coffee station. Usually, therefore, the suggestions were kind of routine. *Can we possibly get a blend with a little hazelnut in it? Just once in a while?* Even if Dolly Halloran hated the vanilla hazelnut variety that Ellie later selected, the suggestion in this instance had met with general favor in the office, bringing good cheer to the lounge area.

Ellie Knight-Cameron was thirty-four, and she was a bit

heavy for her age, or maybe it was just that despite years of workout regimens and exotic diets she had never once resembled a svelte, cosmopolitan type of woman, and she was a little self-conscious about this, despite her brown ringlets, which took an awful lot of work to maintain, and the mole above her upper lip that she thought was one of her best features. Her eyes were as gray as flagstones. She had an easy smile. People liked her, just not in that flinging-off-clothes kind of way.

Ellie's hyphenated surname, to broach a sore subject, was the creation of her parents, who were as yet unmarried. These free spirits had met in the early seventies, out in the Sun Belt. The conception of Ellie Knight-Cameron, according to the story, had taken place during a festival gig by the venerable Allman Brothers Band. There'd been a particularly adventurous solo by Dickey Betts. In the far distance, beneath a tattered blanket, love conjoined the not terribly illustrious families Knight and Cameron.

Every Saturday, Ellie cleaned her apartment in Rye, and she started in the bedroom and worked her way north in order to avoid disturbing her cat, Nails, for the longest possible time. Ellie had ridiculously strong feelings about her vacuum cleaner, which was British, purple, and designed by an aeronautical engineer. Her excitement about vacuuming depressed her, though if you are going to be depressed about your enthusiasms, you should at least have a reliable vacuum cleaner as consolation prize.

On Saturdays she cleaned, and then she went to the organic market, and then she tried to arrange pastimes that involved her friends from the office or from college. She'd gone to school in the early nineties, those go-go years, as far away from the Southwest as she could get, which turned out to be Westchester County. What she liked to do with her friends from college—most of whom had crazy, arty ambitions—was play miniature golf. She also loved minor league baseball. At some hazy point in the future she intended to learn the tango.

Because Ellie Knight-Cameron was orderly in her habits and in her thinking, she'd been a natural hire for Kolodny and Kolodny. The name of the firm was a little misleading, actually, because there was only one Kolodny, and that was Duane, who had long ago hoped to lure his boy, Mark, into the business. Mark had gone into real estate instead, though he nonetheless presumed to inherit the business, perhaps so he could sell it off. Duane Kolodny had begun life as a contractor in Fairfield County, but he'd become fed up with the lawlessness and Darwinism of contracting. The gravel business was controlled by the mob, the cement business was controlled by the mob, the building permits were controlled by the politicians, the politicians were on the take, and so forth. Duane was a low-key person. He'd settled on insurance because it was pragmatic. He didn't have to sell too hard; he just had to believe in his product. Which was another way of saying that Duane believed that you should take care of yourself and your family and move gingerly through life, on the lookout for trouble.

According to Ellie Knight-Cameron's K&K psychological profiling, it was extremely unlikely that Duane Kolodny, who was seventy years old and couldn't bring himself to retire, had written the petulant suggestion about the lane closures on the Merritt Parkway. Duane kept to himself. For example, no one had known about the problems between Duane and his wife, not until that rash of days when his office door was very firmly closed. Duane had emerged one afternoon complaining of allergies and gone home early. Not long after, he was a bachelor.

It wasn't clear that Duane even knew there *was* a suggestion box. The aforementioned Dolly Halloran, Duane's executive assistant, knew there was one. She'd lobbied for it in the first place. Ellie herself knew about it, of course. She checked it every day or so. As for the rest of the staff, they knew of the suggestion box because it was sitting right there, enfolded in pink wrapping paper, by the coffee machine. It had originally served as a box of bathroom tissues and would have been recycled as such had Ellie not plucked it from obscurity and festooned it.

She looked closer at the offending suggestion. There was the *goddamned* part of it: *If they're going to close lanes on the parkway, they ought to actually repair the goddamned road.* The word *goddamned*, more forceful than its rather dainty abbreviation *damn*, was kind of antique when you thought about it, a little bit like something you'd say if you were an older person. But there just weren't that many older people at K&K, not counting Duane. *Goddamned.* Women didn't say it that much, or maybe they only said it in the 1950s, when it was arguably the curse of choice, or so Ellie believed. Her mother used to say it to her when she was a girl. Ellie's teenage attempts to wear exactly what everyone else was wearing to school were something her mother swore about with muscular decisiveness. One time Ellie just put her foot down, so to speak, saying she *had* to have leg warmers, whereupon her mother told her she was just like *some rich bitch from the goddamned suburbs.*

K&K employed nine eager, self-motivated professionals, in addition to Ellie. Of the nine employees, seven were women. One was Duane Kolodny and one was Neil Rubinstein, who couldn't possibly be a heterosexual type of man, because there was no sexual wattage coming off him, no romantic chemistry, no nothing. How did the women of the office come up with these sorts of hypotheses? How did they have the time? Neil was responsible for bookkeeping and payroll, and he kept to himself, and when you looked deeply into Neil's eyes, you saw they were like the molded plastic eyes of a stuffed animal.

Neil was interested in weather patterns. If you had to pass Neil Rubinstein on the way to the bathroom three times a day, which you probably did, because his cubicle was right *by* the bathroom, then you wanted to have something to offer him. Neil followed the Weather Channel through the regional forecast two or three times before bed, this was assured. He could discourse about airport closings. If a freak storm in Detroit had grounded much of the Northwest Airlines fleet, Neil would know, and he was always excited when the weather news was particularly bad, even if in his case excitement was hard to gauge. If three inches of rain were promised, and maximum sustained winds topping fifty miles an hour, it would be a very good day for Neil Rubinstein.

What's more, Neil dressed as though he had never yet been allowed to change clothes after Hebrew lessons, and his shirts always had French cuffs, and the payroll checks were always on time, and there was never a problem with accounts payable or receivable. Neil Rubinstein was a knot that resisted untangling. Ellie Knight-Cameron believed, therefore, that Neil was very likely the person who'd typed out the suggestion about the lane closures, at least because *goddamned* seemed more masculine, and Neil seemed as if he was maybe a tyrant secreted away in the outfit of an inoffensive accountant. Maybe there was a body bricked up in his cellar, or a series of bodies, or maybe he'd had an unfortunate episode of frottage with an elementary school teacher.

There was just one problem with her theory: Neil Rubinstein didn't drive.

Recently, Ellie had been in a Greek diner in Riverside, a couple of towns over. Above her booth, above her duct-taped vinyl banquette, hung a reproduction of a painting of Athens, Greece. Forget the rest of the interior. Don't even worry about the circumstances. A coincidence is when two clients can be sourced to the same finder, or when two brokers woo the same institutional prospect. This time the coincidence was as follows: she'd seen the *same* artistic reproduction of Athens on the night of her college graduation! What an eventful night that had been! A boy kissed her and told her that no woman was ever as beautiful. And the same picture hung nearby, a depiction of some rubble in Athens or Rome. Ellie Knight-Cameron had definitely kissed a boy, no one could dispute it, and the boy was called Eric Banks, and Eric Banks was a little bit hirsute, and he sported a chronically strained expression. He believed the worst about people and events. Most nights, Eric Banks was hunched over a viola that he couldn't bow properly.

Yet when Eric spoke to Ellie about all the strange music

that he liked—a guitar played with chopsticks, a piano plucked from the inside—it was like he was shedding his papery exterior. She enjoyed listening to him. When he felt better she felt better. It went back and forth like that for a couple of weeks, until the night of graduation. They were together when they shed their graduation gowns, when they threw their tasseled hats into a big pile by the coatrack. Together they were sitting in the reception hall where the party was in full swing. The music was incredibly loud, and Eric was worried about his hearing. He wore earplugs on the train into the city; he wore them on planes, at rock shows, at amusement parks. Ellie shouted in one of Eric's temporarily deaf ears that she thought something great was going to happen to him.

And Ellie Knight-Cameron wasn't just believing in Eric in order to believe. They looked away, oppositely, and while she pretended to be deep in metaphysical speculation, watching dancers flail in the center of the room, she happened to glance at a painting on the wall. It was a painting of the Acropolis in Athens, or some kind of ruin from early western civilization, which made sense, right? This was graduation. Ancient Greece, higher education, Athens. When she faced Eric again, he was reaching out to her, he was fitting his callused hand around her chin, pressing his mouth against hers. The taste was of hummus, Dr Pepper, and green olives. Later, she wished she had made love with him, because you should take advantage of the chances you get. They kissed and then they held each other. The dancers flailed. Eric told her that she was a beautiful woman. They made oaths. She went back to Arizona for the summer. Eric went to music school in Boston.

And then, depressingly, they didn't really stay in touch.

So: it was a melancholy night at the diner. In fact, Ellie had been trying to talk with her mother by cell phone about her luck with the male of the species. Her mother was the wrong person to ask. "Why don't you buy some sexy outfits and go out to a bar or something?" This from the self-described feminist who'd borne three out-of-wedlock children by three different self-employed men. Ellie's brother, Len, was doing a short stay in the Big House for selling marijuana to high school students. Her older sister was living in Taos, tattooing.

What she was meant to be doing at the Greek diner in Riverside was writing a want ad. There was a vacancy among the brokers at K&K. There was always a vacancy. K&K could carry four brokers but had trouble keeping four on board. People had priorities that did not include loyalty to their small-business employers. So Ellie Knight-Cameron was taken up with the process of advertising, of interviewing applicants, of making hiring recommendations. In a company like K&K there wasn't a genuine *director of personnel*. Ellie was certified in computer networking and telephone routing. She had opinions about desk chairs. When Ellie had the applicants narrowed down to two, she'd send them along to Duane.

She was impressed, at first, with a guy from Greenwich. His name was Chris Grady. He hadn't managed to go to a great college like a lot of young men from Greenwich, not even a midlevel college, really, but she believed on the basis of their telephone conversation that Chris had *the selling gene*. Duane had told her to look out for this. It was about energy, it was about enthusiasm, it was about hunger, it was about patriotism, it was about vision, it was about the big picture, the wide spectrum, it was about refusing to say *no*.

Not long after, Chris visited the office. Chris wore light blue socks that matched his handkerchief. This may have been a strike against him. Excessive matching. There was a shy way that Chris folded and refolded his hands in his lap, even as he was displaying his thousand-watt smile. He was a beautiful young man from Greenwich and he wore a suit from Brooks Brothers or from some other preppy haberdasher. Chris probably had a brother who was better than he was at everything. This older brother tortured Chris and never let him win at any game.

During the first interview, Ellie Knight-Cameron asked Chris if he had suggestions for her about how K&K might improve its business. Chris didn't hesitate.

"Acquisition," Chris said. And then, emboldened, "Economies of scale. Insurance is a good business, and it's, uh. There's always going to be, everyone needs insurance, but you could really, uh, go head-to-head with some of your competitors, you know, and you could, then you squeeze them out of market share, and then you'd, uh, you know, you'd have more market share. Here in the . . . the . . . Connecticut area. Because then you wouldn't, uh, you wouldn't have as many competitors. Here."

"Great!" Ellie said.

She introduced Chris around. She introduced him to Angie Roehmer, Astrid Lang, and Bonnie Stevenson, these being the brokers who remained; she introduced him to Maureen Jones, the mail room worker, and Christina

Niccoli, the filing clerk just out of high school who harbored dreams of becoming a buyer at one of the big department stores. Ellie passed right by Neil Rubinstein. Then there was the enigma, Annie Goldberg, who was supposed to be a part-time researcher for K&K but who was also, everybody knew, a compulsive gambler. She was often missing on one of her sprees at the Indian casinos.

The women in the office would prefer to have another man around. Gender equity was a motivator in the workplace. This was what Duane always said. Ellie believed him. When she was young, she'd thought she would be a psychologist. Not the kind where you did experiments on rats but the kind where you got to interact with people and hear about their lives. Though she hadn't followed through on her dream, her psychological studies were excellent preparation for interacting with her crazy family and the people in her workplace.

A strange thing happened. With Chris from Greenwich. During the office tour, she showed him the new wall-to-wall that they'd laid down in the lounge–conference room. (Dusty rose, because suggestions in the suggestion box had indicated that this color would make happy the majority of K&K employees.) Then, after she showed him the carpet, she showed him the suggestion box. This caused her, of course, to remember what she'd mostly forgotten, that bizarre suggestion, the one about the Merritt Parkway. She never had figured out who could possibly have written it. All she had done was rule out Duane and then cast some suspicion on Neil Rubinstein before moving on to her daily tasks, which were more important. But as she was explaining the suggestion box to Chris from Greenwich—"This is where people in the office are free to come up with suggestions about how to streamline the office in order to make it more efficient and responsive"—Chris snickered a little bit. There was no other word. He sounded like a cicada, and his shoulders trembled in a masculine, self-satisfied way. That was when she really looked at his, what do you call those, those little beard things. Just on the bottom part of his chin. The beard thing proved that Chris would be exactly the type to put something dreadful in the K&K suggestion box.

Chris *couldn't* have written the suggestion about the cones and the lane closures, of course, because she had never heard of him nor even seen his name on a résumé until just three days before, and this was his first visit to the office. Yet she was certain, somehow, that he'd done it. And that meant, to Ellie Knight-Cameron, that there was something amiss with this applicant. He wasn't telling her the whole truth about himself. In fact, at that very moment she became passionate about the other applicant, a disabled girl called Lisa Weltz. One of Lisa's arms was a little withered thing, like Bob Dole's arm. Still, Lisa was ambitious, presentable, and smart.

It wasn't that Ellie Knight-Cameron never listened to her mother, counselor on all things romantic, when her mother told her to dress herself up and go to the bars. She had done so, just as advised, in certain desperate moods. She would go to the bars and strike up a perfectly nice conversation with a bartender. One time she met a sweet paralegal called Rhonda, with whom she stayed in touch. The two of them, in outfits so tight that breathing was out of the question, sat at one end of the bar, gabbing about everything there was to gab about. Later Rhonda came to K&K for her personal insurance needs. And Angie Roehmer split the commission with Ellie, which was really generous.

The complicated allure of singles bars gave Ellie acid indigestion. She found herself wearing things she would never wear and thinking about cleavage. She put up her hair, she used a lot of eyeliner, she thought, *There are so many things that indicate that this* is *the night: the moon is bright, the air is crisp, and lost causes are not lost on nights like this one.* She tried to convince herself. It was spring, after all. She had recently won the office pool on the Oscars. The Red Sox were in first, even if it was just the beginning of the season. She went to the bars in a state of hopefulness. Later she felt crushed. When the morning came around she still had the pillow over her head and she was convinced that there were bugs crawling on her and the room was painted with fungi. There was no good reason that she should go outside.

The night after Chris Grady's interview, she was fed up enough to go barhopping. She went to one of the watering holes downtown, a block from the homely modernist train station, a bar where the SUVs rolled up, and professional men and women from the offices tumbled out in search of drinks with parasols in them. She'd called Rhonda and told her that she might go barhopping, but the plan never developed the crust of genuine intention. Sometimes two smart girls together just embarrassed each other.

Ellie stood at the bar, breathing shallowly, in a skirt that looked as if it had been sprayed directly onto her from a vat of petrochemicals. She ordered a screwdriver, though she almost never drank anything strong. Then another. Then the evening slowed. Olives were being placed in the mouths of lipsticked women by their opposite numbers, and it was as if asteroids were rolling imperceptibly through space. Glasses that were plunked down on the bar sounded like kettle drums. Hoarse laughter rang out from the interior of a canyon. Ellie imagined a peacock striding toward the bar and screeching its mating call. Eventually, this bird would display its ridiculous plumage.

Out of the crowd, a man. A sideburned sort of a man. He shouted something in her ear, but she couldn't hear. She could tell, though, just from his style what he *wasn't* saying: he wasn't saying could he have her number, please, or would it be possible to get to know her better? Ellie nodded vacantly. Then he gently tugged at her elbow, and she followed him toward the booths in the crypt beyond the bar, where the light from the overhead bulbs glowed with the dim blue of industrial subbasements. She found herself, against her better judgment, jammed into a booth with three or four football enthusiasts and two or three ditzy girls who had half the inhibitions she had. Among the predatory individuals assembled was none other than Chris Grady.

She said, "What a surprise!"

"How about that!"

"Well, um, do you come here often?" How long would she have to formulate this inoffensive banter? "My friend Rhonda—" She pointed toward the bar, though Rhonda was not actually present.

"Right," Chris said.

One of Chris's pals inquired, "You work at the—?"

"Insurance," Ellie said. "Chris was—"

"Yeah," Chris Grady said. There was a lot of nodding. A

conversation followed about which was the best kind of bar, the dingy kind or the *really* dingy kind. Ellie had no opinion. She could imagine bulldozing all of the bars in the Stamford area. Civilization would continue. The best kind of bar was one where you didn't get attacked before, during, or after your appearance there. The best kind of bar was one where you didn't go home feeling you'd been emptied of everything that was substantial about you. The best kind of bar was one where you didn't feel like a yearbook summary of yourself or like a bunch of measurements. There was no such bar. Even though the conversation was not, you know, particularly malevolent, Ellie felt again that there was something she didn't trust about Chris Grady. He talked about cars a lot. And sale prices of things.

Not two days later, she got to work early, like she almost always did, opened the suggestion box, having neglected it for a number of weeks, and found: *You ought to throw this fucking coffee machine out the window and run over it with a car.*

She reread it a couple of times to be sure she was seeing what she believed she was seeing. *This fucking machine. Fucking machine. Fucking. Fucking. Fucking.* The decorum that had been characterized by *goddamned* in the earlier suggestion had now given way to the vulgar word *fucking.* Of course, it was also true that in this case the suggestion did fall under Ellie Knight-Cameron's professional jurisdiction. She was responsible for the coffee machine. Bad coffee, in her view, was almost a public service, because it gave people a problem to solve. If weather, traffic, baseball, and coffee were universally agreed upon, if everyone decided these things had been made perfect and harmonious, then there would be no reason to use human language at all. People would walk around like monks, saying nothing.

Interestingly, there was an automotive implication in both of the offending messages. In the first, it was about traffic on the Merritt Parkway, and in the second, there was the suggestion that someone should *run over* the coffee machine. With a motor vehicle. Whoever was writing the messages was certainly interested in cars, or had a car, or was a regular rider in a car. Users of mass transit were out.

Astrid Lang, for example. Astrid's refusal to drive some-how went with her mouse brown hair, her bowed legs, and her grown son who still lived at home with her. She was sort of anxious about things, and that was maybe why Astrid worked in insurance. She hadn't fallen into the business by chance. Astrid had strong feelings about disaster. She braced for im-pact. She was good at persuading people that they didn't have enough insurance. Who knew what was going to happen in this era of climatic change and earthquakes and tsunamis and hurricanes? Astrid was convincing about these things because she was worried about asbestos in her house, or else her boiler was making that awful noise, or one of the tree limbs was go-ing to come down, and global warming was going to bring about a precipitous ice age and a forty-foot storm surge.

Ellie stood sentinel-like by the suggestion box. She was still holding the piece of paper in her hand, a piece of un-lined scrap paper, when Astrid Lang happened by. It oc-curred to Ellie that she should hide the suggestion, and it was this impulse that reminded her: she had told no one about the first note. The suggestion about the parkway. She hadn't told a soul about it, and why not? She tried to think back on what she had done in the weeks that had passed. She tried to retrace her steps. Was there some kind of shame associated with these notes? Because it was *her* suggestion box? She was the one who believed strongly in the democratic values of the suggestion box. She was the one who had wrapped it in pink wrapping paper. She was the one who emptied it. It was as if the first note was addressed *to her*.

She wished Astrid good morning too loudly. She smiled brightly.

"What do you have there?" Astrid asked. Astrid was on the alert for any event, any snippet of gossip, any off-hours visit or collective dinner that could be said to have excluded her, even though she rarely attended when invited and never offered invitations in return.

"Look at this, Astrid," Ellie said. She felt a bit of relief in handing it over, in making the suggestion a public problem, even if just with Astrid.

With a brisk certainty, Astrid fetched lavender-framed reading glasses from her weather-beaten purse. She read the message over carefully, penetratingly, before handing it back. Her expression never changed.

"That's overreacting."

"I'll say," Ellie said.

"It's typed," Astrid said.

Which ruled out certain people. For example, Bonnie Stevenson, who filled out most of her forms by hand and who made Christina type them into the system for her. Bonnie's nails were too long for typing, that was her argument on the subject. She just couldn't type, and that was the end of the discussion.

"Did I ever tell you," Ellie said to Astrid, "what my father would do to us if we used that word?"

"What word?"

"*That* word. The *f* word."

"No," Astrid said, "you never told me. But I don't really have time."

Astrid was on her way to Duane's office. She was intent upon the Duane Kolodny gatekeeper, Dolly Halloran, to whom she would make clear her need to see Duane. After which she would wait as long as it took. Duane was never available. If you wanted to take up something confidential or important with him, the moment to do it was right when he got in. Astrid knew this.

Ellie stood by the suggestion box for a while, shaken, as though standing by it would persuade it to pity her, and then out of desperation she turned her attention to some of the things posted on a nearby company bulletin board. A note from Duane directing the staff to use express mail services sparingly. A handbill about a time-share in a condo on Sea Island. How to recognize a choking incident.

In fact, at that very moment, Astrid Lang was resigning from K&K. Astrid had been on her way to quit when Ellie stopped her for her suggestions about the offending note. That Astrid had said nothing about quitting did not surprise Ellie. The employees of K&K had precious little information about Astrid Lang.

Astrid hadn't let on that she was going to quit, nor did she let on about what she was going to do next, how she was going to pay her monthly bills, and, except for telling Ellie that she could keep her commemorative mug from the AAIB conference in Cincinnati, Astrid left behind no sign that she had ever been at K&K at all. Her exit was fully accomplished by lunch.

In the PM, Lisa Weltz and Chris Grady came back for additional interviews. The mood in the office was expectant but worried. The office pulsed with the electricity that is incipient change among personnel. The women suddenly were restless in their client contacts, unable to focus on new solicitations. The women of K&K now seemed to favor Lisa Weltz, though they didn't want to risk irritating Duane, king of all he surveyed, who, it was rumored, preferred Chris. Never mind that K&K could have used both of the candidates.

During her big interview with Duane, in the afternoon, Lisa Weltz had complained about K&K compliance with the Americans with Disabilities Act, noting (this was what Dolly reported) that this noncompliance was likely affecting K&K's ability to attract large institutional clients. They had no ramp to the office and no railing in the bathroom. The plumbing fixtures needed attention. Everyone in the office, Lisa Weltz observed, was able-bodied. And having delivered these pronouncements, Lisa Weltz cradled her withered arm under her breasts.

Duane, the way he told it, when they were all gathered in the conference room, tried to be polite about Lisa W., but in the end he'd made up his mind quickly, noting that he would never avoid hiring someone because she had a disability. He would, however, avoid hiring someone because she was sour, had crumbs on her blouse, and exhibited bad manners at a pivotal juncture in the interview process.

Chris Grady took Astrid's position as broker, effective the next morning.

. . .

Further weeks passed, and Ellie knew what this meant. The passage of time meant that it was likely the perpetrator of the creepy suggestion box messages, the two messages that violated the civility of the K&K offices, was none other than Astrid Lang. And yet there was something mysterious about this. There was something inexplicable about a woman who had no car making hotheaded suggestions about lane closures on the Merritt Parkway. Would a woman who mostly drank tea complain about the coffee? However, inductively speaking, all the evidence suggested that Lang was the perpetrator. Therefore, Ellie Knight-Cameron forgot about the suggestion box, except once a week when she would reach absently into the bottom of the message receptacle to realize that once again it had gone unused. All was well.

Here's the story Ellie had never told Astrid. The story about her father and the *f* word. Her parents, when she was young, had unusual parenting ideas. For example, you didn't have to go to school if you didn't feel like it. Everyone should sleep together in the same bed. You should skinny-dip with your family. You should tell your family about any romantic escapades that you had; it was your obligation. And if you were going to use drugs or drink, you should do these things *with* your family, so that these activities could be properly supervised. It was only later that Ellie found out many parents had quite different ideas.

And even though her parents agreed upon these unusual parenting principles, there were far more numerous principles on which they disagreed. For example, her father *hated* the *f* word. If anyone used the *f* word, if her brother used the *f* word, her father would become extremely agitated. It was not, her father said, tugging nervously on his beard, that he had any problem with the activity described by the word in question. Anyone who wanted to perform that particular activity should do so, according to the rules of consent, whenever he or she wanted to do it, with whomever he or she wanted. Anyone could use whatever part of his or her body he or she wanted to use, her father went on, as long as this body part gave her pleasure. The skin was the largest organ on the human body. This was what was good about life, the moment in which skin brushed up against skin. The little skin receptors of delight created cascading sensations in the chakras and in the perineum. In conclusion, a person should not use this *f* word to describe what she or he was doing, her father said, because to use this *f* word was to denigrate a beautiful and holy act in which waves cascaded to and from the perineum. By denigrating the act you were denigrating one of the few perfect things about being a human animal in this disappointing world, and Ellie's father would not tolerate it.

Red-handed, that's how her father caught her brother using the word. In fact, it was one of many times her brother called Ellie a "fucking idiot." Soon the punishment was meted out. Her father made her brother read through the dictionary, and not one of those little paperback dictionaries but actually an old mossy copy of *Webster's Third International*, after which her brother was *tasked* with writing down every single adjective in the *f* section of the dictionary, so that her brother might be able to call up possible alternatives to "fucking idiot," such as "felonious idiot," or "fastidious idiot," or "fungible idiot," or "funereal idiot," or "fetishistic idiot." Furious idiot, free-spirited idiot, fiduciary idiot, floral idiot, fucaceous idiot, foehnlike idiot, fluorescent idiot, foliiform idiot, facetious idiot, falsetto idiot, funicular idiot, feathery idiot, freelance idiot, fugitive idiot. It took her brother half a day to perform this expiation, during which time he wasn't allowed to go to school. He went through three number two pencils, his hand developed a horrible cramp, and Ellie felt triumphant. A triumph that would be short-lived.

That night her mother came back from interviewing migrant farm workers, and she took one look at the pages and pages of dictionary entries Ellie's brother had copied out onto a legal pad and began calling Ellie's father an "uptight prude asshole."

During the period of weeks when there was no action at the K&K suggestion box, Ellie was in fact making ready to visit her family in Arizona, a trip she did not want to make. Her father had called to tell her that her mother had turned up, after going missing for several days, in Tempe, a town that Ellie found particularly melancholy. Ellie's mother had been detained by the authorities on a charge of drunk and disorderly behavior, somewhere near the campus of the state university, where she was not registered for classes.

Chris Grady demonstrated, in his first months on the job, that he was a man on the go. The offices rang out with the banter of Chris and Duane in the executive office in the mornings, talking about the golf they had played, about the basketball tournament they had bet on, or about an impending football game. At first this fraternity seemed like a good thing, based on Duane Kolodny's theory that a mixing of the sexes resulted in a productive workplace. Chris was always in the office early, before Ellie arrived, and when she threw her trench coat over the couch in the lounge and turned on the coffee machine, Chris always called out to her, "Hey, babe, how the hell are you!"

To which she replied, "Don't call me babe!"

Nonessential employees were the first to go. Christina Niccoli, the filing clerk, decided that she needed business school in order to realize her dream of working as a buyer for one of the larger department stores. Ellie herself wrote the advertisement for the *Advocate* in which they invited applications to replace Christina, experience a plus. She returned to the restaurant with the painting of the Acropolis in order to draft the text. Christina was a sweet kid, and when Ellie conducted her exit interview, Christina complained that Duane didn't seem to care about the office the way he used to. In the old days—they weren't so far in the past—Duane would occasionally call a halt to the business day and take them all out for ice cream.

Then, Annie Goldberg, the staff researcher and unrepentant gambler, disappeared. And it was a few days before anyone even noticed. Ellie asked Dolly Halloran if she'd seen Annie, and Dolly said truculently, "Who?" Of course, in the present business environment, the big decisions were made by the parent company—about rates, the deductibles, that sort of thing. Clients had begun complaining about the wind deduction, especially on the region's marshy coast. Hurricane season was longer with the greenhouse effect. And there was the risk of terrorist activity. Annie used to keep statistics on claims, but computers could do all that now. People and their foibles just clotted up the system. The big imponderables appeared on the horizon, wrought their havoc, and left claimants to reassemble shattered lives. Price tags were in the tens of billions. Kolodny & Kolodny didn't control the Atlantic hurricane season or the winter cold snaps. Didn't matter what a bunch of salespeople in Stamford thought about anything; they could all drive off a cliff. Their families would collect.

How many people had worked at K&K in the twenty or thirty years that Duane Kolodny had managed the company? Maybe he no longer cared. The only constant, besides Duane, was Dolly Halloran. How could a woman with such a hoarse, acid laugh be called Dolly? Who'd ever thought she was a Dolly? She was too skinny. The skin hung off her elbows. She penciled in her eyebrows. Dolly favored tissues in little plastic packets, and she was always using these tissues to dab at her rheumy eyes. People said that Dolly had been Duane's mistress, or at least Bonnie Stevenson said so. Yet this implied that at one time Dolly had loved someone.

What really concerned Ellie Knight-Cameron was not whether Duane and Dolly had conducted a bittersweet office affair. What concerned Ellie was that Astrid had now left the company, and Christina was gone and Annie Goldberg was gone, and with Annie went the room freshener that she used in her cubicle, one of those plug-in jobs. A hint of cinnamon. Christina had listened to music on her headphones. She was always tapping on things. She wore too many earrings. Christina was pear shaped, but in a cute way. Considering that Ellie Knight-Cameron, according to statistically sound methodologies, had in prior weeks removed Duane and Neil Rubinstein from consideration in the matter of the suggestion box, and considering further that Christina and Annie had now abandoned the K&K family, and discounting Astrid Lang, that left as potential suggestion box culprits only Angie, Dolly, Bonnie Stevenson, or Maureen Jones. These people had opportunity and access, but did they have motive?

Angie Roehmer cornered her by the water cooler. Down the hall from the bathroom. They were both working late. Business was so good Duane was thinking of expanding. Ellie was trying to get prices on a larger suite in the same office building. This despite the fact that they had never hired a fourth broker and the rest of the staff was actually shrinking. It had been raining for days. A yowling stray cat in the parking lot had scuttled all attempts to locate and muzzle it.

It was all about Chris Grady. Everything was different for Chris Grady, Angie Roehmer said. Things had been easier before Chris Grady. There were certain things that women did for one another, Angie said. One thing they did was they tried not to be cruel, and they tried to remember to clean the dishes in the sink in the lounge if the dishes piled up. They didn't leave old coffee cups around with a three-day-old paste in the bottom. They didn't ignore one another. They weren't out for another person's job. Even when the women were disrespectful to one another, they tried to do it in a graceful way where nobody had to go to the bathroom and cry. And if someone *did* have to go and cry, they'd offer her a hug after.

"I heard him in there, and I think he's trying to get people fired. He's trying to make us look bad." Angie filled yet another paper cup with water from the cooler and downed it in a swallow. "You think I don't notice stuff?" Crushing the cup emphatically. "I wasn't hired yesterday."

Angie suggested they booby-trap Chris Grady's clients. He was offering discounts that he shouldn't have been offering. On bulk enrollments. He took days off without marking the time sheets, which meant he was stealing from the company. He was always going sailing or waterskiing with his richer and more successful relatives. They could catch him in it, and things would return to their earlier, calmer state, where women coexisted peaceably, working together for the common good.

"Angie," Ellie said, "I can't do anything like that. That wouldn't be right. I—"

Look at the organization chart! Read her job description! She was just an office manager. She ordered carpet remnants. She telephoned plumbers.

"I always thought you were a goody-goody," Angie said.

How to make sense of this embittered remark? Well, for one thing, Angie's daughter was going to college soon, and Ellie happened to know that her kid barely spoke to Angie, the single parent. Ellie had watched this daughter as she went through her sullen adolescent patch before graduating into a full-fledged hatred of her mom, which had been much on display at both the summer office picnic and at the Christmas party. Last Christmas, the daughter, whose name was Maria, got sloppy drunk, and later, when everyone was climbing into their cars behind the steak house, Maria could be heard berating her mother: *You're so fucking boring, why don't you go take a boring pill or something. All I ever wanted was a little fun.* Ellie gazed at Angie, and she saw herself in another fifteen years, desperate to hang on to a job she didn't care about so she could pay for college for a daughter who hated her.

She may have been wrong about Chris Grady and Astrid Lang, but now she was right. It *was* Angie Roehmer. No question. Angie was the one who had written the suggestions. How could Ellie have missed it before? Angie was willing to do anything. She was willing to say whatever she had to say to protect her small, miserable family. You controlled or you were controlled, and if you didn't control, if you saw life and liberty slipping beyond your grasp, then you began doing things you would regret later, like beating up on your girl's soccer coach or embezzling company funds. You grabbed a Starbucks employee by her green apron and told her you were going to knock all her teeth out if she ever again put whipped cream on your half-decaf mochaccino.

Angie's inexplicable sick-out started soon after the unpleasant conversation above. Duane Kolodny couldn't understand it, because Angie was one of his best workers. He'd hired her away from a dead-end job long before Ellie had joined K&K. Why would Angie go unreliable on him? Dolly covered for her for a few days, and then Dolly told Duane, or this was what she told Ellie, that Angie just couldn't take another minute in an office that featured boy wonder Chris Grady. "Oh, bullcrap," Duane had said. "He's our number one earner." In fact, Chris was one of the top earners in the whole region for K&K's parent company. And he was about to pitch the head of personnel at a local Fortune 500 conglomerate on their entire health insurance plan. If he got the account, it would secure K&K until well after Duane Kolodny's demise.

Ellie was meant to conduct a new round of job interviews the next day. It was a rainy, angry morning in late summer, and the applicants would probably be coming in late. She took off her raincoat and her hat and put them in the coat closet, and she pulled the umbrella stand out of the closet and set it by the front door. Her duck-handled umbrella was comical, protruding above the rim of the faux-wood-veneer umbrella stand as if it didn't want her to leave it behind. She loved ducks.

The unpleasant smell coming from the minifridge was as it always was. There was a leak by the front door where Ellie eventually set a metal bowl to collect the rain. And, after much disuse, the suggestion box, it seemed, contained a suggestion, one folded into eighths or sixteenths by some obsessive party. Here were the words of the new suggestion that Ellie now held in her hand: *Worldwide revolution now. Throw off your chains.*

The stress *was* beginning to get to her. The stress of the office, of the office that was changing so fast during the Chris Grady regime. You could see it all, as plain as the cancerous mole on your forearm. This piece of paper she held was practically a Communist suggestion, like you'd expect from someone who had read too much Marx in college. Still, Ellie couldn't seem to talk about it with anyone else. She couldn't seem to bring the suggestion box up with Dolly or Bonnie, because now that Angie was on sick leave or fired or whatever she was, now there were only three plausible authors, and two of them were her remaining friends in the company, namely Dolly Halloran and Bonnie Stevenson.

She couldn't talk about it, and so she lay awake at night, thinking about the idea of *worldwide revolution*. If she could just figure it out, if she could just slot the right people into the equation, then she could do something useful for this company she had so ably served for six years.

Her back really hurt a couple days a week—a throbbing, disquieting pain—and she couldn't seem to find a desk chair in the catalogue of office furniture that had the right kind of lumbar support. There was a trainer at the gym she kind of liked, and he would have recommendations for an ergonomically designed chair, but she hadn't spoken to him about it, and she kept imagining something was going to happen to her on the StairMaster. She would be ground up in it. People got swallowed whole by escalators, after all. People who'd just gone to the mall to buy shoelaces.

She called her father, told him she was looking forward to coming home, though this was not true. He told Ellie that he'd heard her mother had been released from the detox. And she hadn't answered his telephone calls, he said. While this was not an unusual situation, since they were unmarried and separated, it was worrisome. Ellie told her father she just wasn't getting what she needed from her job. Her house, she said, was fully outfitted with furniture that you assembled from kits. She bought foods that were low in calories, and she tried to eat only organic things, and everything was straightened up, she had straightened everything up, she liked to have the magazines on the coffee table at right angles, she told her father, she understood that celebrities were marrying and divorcing at alarming rates, and that people would do anything to be on television. But this was not, it turned out, enough.

"Honey," he said, "try volunteering."

Everyone had stayed in the Southwest except the youngest child, and in the interrogative sun, the unrelenting sun of the desert summer, they had their upheavals and their difficulties, rarely regretting. Meanwhile, she was here in this state where she was always expecting to round a corner and find a scorched valley below her, empty as far as she could see. She was expecting vistas of cacti and the sounds of coyotes, but in the East everything was claustrophobic and heartbroken, especially after the third suggestion.

Bonnie Stevenson announced that she was going into business with Angie Roehmer. The two of them intended to start a boutique that competed directly with K&K on some large accounts. They had a catchy name for the operation, which was Reconstruction Inc., and they had a really great logo, sort of an antebellum southern porch in a pale blue, on the top of the letterhead. The business plan had been in place for some time. Maybe the insurance sector needed to be reconstructed, the way these two campy entrepreneurs saw it. Rates spiraled upward and drove everything in the region, drove the way people did everything they did, the way they walked through a building lobby or played on a swing set. You could easily trip in a mall stairwell and disfigure yourself. A scary ride at the amusement park might cause you to go into a tailspin of depression and affect your earnings potential.

It was Bonnie and Angie, and they were in it together, they had taken the whole office for a ride with their negative attitudes and their hatred of men. Ellie Knight-Cameron wasn't one of those people; she kind of loved men. At any rate, the women's conspiracy was figured out, or it would have been all figured out if Ellie had not found yet another suggestion in the suggestion box *the very next day*, the first full day after Bonnie left the firm, having been ordered out by Duane, ordered off the premises and her laptop taken away from her and her pens and paper clips impounded.

Still, when you tallied only these dramatic incidents at K&K, you missed the rhythm of work, the flow of how people lived, which was in eight-hour increments, or really in four-hour increments because of lunch. Everyone went out for lunch at a place up the block, even if the cappuccino machine was on the fritz. The women of K&K, back when they were in it together, they all went out. It looked bad if you stayed at your desk for lunch. It looked like you were showing up the other women of K&K by working harder than they were working. This was the unspoken agreement. There was a rhythm of work, and it was all about insuring against the unpredictable. Of course, there were other things that were as difficult as office life: church, local politics, the playground, high school dances, but all Ellie did was work.

Among her interviewees on this particular day was Chris Grady's friend with the sideburns, one Noel Goodrich. The guy she'd met at the bar. He was dressed in khakis, blue blazer, loafers without socks. He had a cyst or something, some kind of permanent skin blemish beside his nose that she hadn't noticed in the light of the bar.

"What are your hobbies?"

"What are my—"

"We feel that hobbies are indicative of keen appreciation for life's—"

"Well, I guess I like to—"

"Cooking?"

"Cooking, *hell no!*" Noel said. "Well, I like to grill. I like to wear the chef's hat outside. Really my hobby is . . . my hobby is, uh, professional sports memorabilia. Shoulder pads, for example. I have signed shoulder pads. Sports have come a long way, you know, in terms of neck injuries."

"You're concerned about neck injuries?"

"And fire prevention."

"What kinds of insurance do you carry?"

"Paternity insurance?" Sensing it was an ineffective joke: "Actually, I don't have any insurance."

"You don't have renter's insurance? Dental insurance?"

His eyes were bloodshot. His future was in the bag. Almost immediately after Goodrich left the office, Chris came over to Ellie's desk. Somehow she had failed to notice earlier that his fingernails were a bit longer than a guy would normally wear them. And there was a strip under his nose where his razor had not performed effectively. Not to mention the damp spot on the elbow of his shirt.

"I can't live with the coffee around here." Maybe he blamed coffee for the spillage on his elbow. "Could you go out and get me my half-decaf mochaccino? With whole milk? And, uh, don't forget a receipt?"

She watched his trim figure bob away. His foppish Hollywood hair. The floppiness of this coiffure elicited contempt in the majority of K&K employees. Ellie would beat on Chris Grady with a stick in the puppet theater production of dreams. Now that the office was really shorthanded, Chris had no natural predator. He didn't have to worry about the office manager. He'd been waiting most of his short, privileged life for this turn of events. He'd sat in the stands at various athletic contests, as though he had webbed feet, cheering his pathologically narcissistic brother, and now was his chance to shine. At last he could begin up-braiding waitresses and using the phrase "Don't you know who I am?"

On the way out the door she stopped in the office lounge and she decided, just because, to check the suggestion box. In retrospect, questions could be raised as to her timing. Had she checked the box on some other day, maybe the result would have been different. Had she been more willing to get Chris's half-decaf mochaccino. Maybe the suggestion box was some kind of context-dependent prognosticatory device. If she'd approached it when feeling upbeat about things, then the box would have provided her with quite different advice.

Because, on the day in question, what the suggestion box found to say to Ellie Knight-Cameron was *All of you should be lined up and shot*.

The first death threat in a person's life is so memorable. Ellie Knight-Cameron had never received a death threat before. In fact, the worst verbal abuse she had experienced in her life involved her brother telling her he was going to kick her ass. She had also, in her youth, been called fat. *Yo, caboose!* Everyone had an opinion: *Was your mother eating for four?* The worse things got—the more weight she put on in high school—the more she was told that this was not going to be tolerated. The more her parents remonstrated with her, the more she snuck downstairs in the quiet part of night and raided the larder. Night was the time when the clamoring in her skull was silenced, when there was no soap opera of her appearance.

How could she be thinking of food? With this murderous suggestion burning a hole in her palm? Yet she *was* thinking about food, however briefly. She couldn't concentrate on the words she'd just read. Her mind glanced off onto other things. In a couple of weeks now she was going to have to fly into Sky Harbor International Airport and face her family. In the meantime, she was cat-sitting the neighbor's cat and it had begun leaving droppings in unusual locations. She stood there holding the typed piece of paper, as if the list of possible interpretations was so vast as to freeze in place any human being. *You should be lined up and shot.*

At some point, Ellie's perturbed mind elected to catch up with her shuddering physique, which was now on its way to Dolly Halloran's cubicle. Her body clutched the note, wadding it, and her mind trailed after, wondering about the legal significance of the moment as she simultaneously catalogued the number and variety of telephone rings on the K&K handsets.

"Dolly," she said, "can you just—"

"Not now."

"I found this in the—"

"Later."

Still, with a kind irritation, Dolly took the note out of Ellie's hand. Ellie noticed, in this instant, that the edges of the note she handed Dolly had been scissored from some larger piece of heavy office bond. The scissoring hadn't been done very well. There were stray hairs, the split ends that you get with an inferior elementary school tool. Therefore, the author of the suggestion was either a lefty, like many poor operators of safety scissors, or he was *simulating* left-handedness in order to confuse.

Dolly's rugged face flushed. She mumbled *What the*—, after which she seemed to drain precipitously of all color. Dolly let out a plangent moan before hugging herself, strangely, as if she were the actual scissor operator and was somehow protecting the arm that had cut out the offending portion of the message. But no, her distress seemed to have little to do with scissoring. Dolly fell to the floor. She called Ellie's name, then Duane's name. In a kind of befuddlement, Ellie heard phones cradled in the other cubicles. She heard Chris Grady getting up from his desk. She heard the new filing clerk, Sheila, tripping on some textured rubber matting as she came running. Then Duane rushed out of his corner office as Dolly was beginning to tremble on the floor. Duane shouted at Ellie to call 911, and Ellie stood there like an idiot before at last reaching down for the phone on Dolly's desk. Yes, yes, someone in the office was having a heart attack, yes, and here was the address, on High Ridge, yes, please, *come quick*. Duane held Dolly's wrist, muttering, and then he climbed athwart her chest as the rest of K&K gathered. Duane pumped away on her rib cage, pausing to force air into her lungs in the time-honored way, then he was back on her chest, and it wasn't hard to see that, yes, he must have been her lover. Now, in the distance, the call of a siren drifted near. It occurred to Ellie to wonder what Dolly was thinking. Was Dolly thinking about her grown children? Were the dead calling to her from their four-star accommodations in the afterlife? Was Dolly regretting that she had written this horrible suggestion and put it in the suggestion box only to be found out by the unsinkable Ellie Knight-Cameron?

Soon paramedics cleared everyone out of the area around Dolly's desk. Only Duane was permitted to stand and nervously watch. Ellie gaped at Duane from over by the coffee station, and the others were peering above the baffles that demarked their cubicles as Dolly Halloran was removed from the premises for her emergency bypass surgery.

It was Duane's decision, taking the rest of the day off, and the cubicles emptied quickly. Ellie Knight-Cameron, in her capacity as office manager, made an outgoing message for the voice mail. She checked her e-mail before leaving the office, in case there was some last task she needed to discharge. And she did have a message, which was: *Ellie, Noel Goodrich is hired. Look after the paperwork. Thanks, Duane.*

She was weeping uninhibitedly as she put on her raincoat, and not because of Dolly's brush with mortality. On the contrary, she was weeping because she now had a practically foolproof method for identifying the demonic author of the most recent suggestion. How had she failed to think of it before? The *font* of the notes. She turned off most of the lights in the empty office, to confound anyone anywhere who might be monitoring her activities. Then, in an interior cubicle where they usually put the filing clerk, she fell into the role of surreptitious system administrator.

First, she examined the default fonts on various people's computers. She noted in passing that a number of K&K employees (Dolly included) did not observe company policy, which held that all the interoffice documents as well as

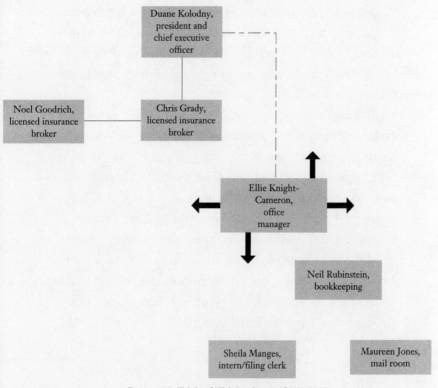

Diagram #2, Kolodny & Kolodny, Inc., as of 8/28/2005

all external correspondence should be composed in the font known as Times New Roman. This was a policy that Ellie Knight-Cameron herself had brought about—with slightly distracted blessings from above.

She ascertained that the last two suggestions in the suggestion box were in a font called Century Gothic, a sans serif typeface. The mere appearance of Century Gothic was at odds with the general policy of Kolody & Kolodny. Sans serif typefaces, Ellie had argued, embodied a disreputable design style from the feel-good seventies. Sans serif typefaces were for organizations that favored unethical business practices. People who used sans serif typefaces would eat frozen diet dinners. These sorts of people subjected chimpanzees to horrific medical testing and they watched television interviews featuring Larry King.

Although she couldn't prove that any locally networked desktop computer had authored the Century Gothic messages, she did feel she was making progress. As the hour ticked around to 8:45 and then 9:30, she riffled through people's drawers and looked at their pens and pencils. Everywhere there were signs that the official K&K orderliness was a sham, a veneer. Maybe she *was* crying about Dolly, of course, or maybe she was crying about not wanting to go back out to Arizona, or maybe she was crying because she was still in the office so late, having read, among other things, private financial data about her friends and coworkers.

"Hello, Eric? It's me, Ellie."

"Ellie?"

"Ellie Knight-Cameron?"

"Oh, wow. Hey. What a surprise!"

"I'm just . . . How are you? I'm just here in the office, working late. So I thought I'd give you a ring and see how you were doing."

"I'm . . . I'm good."

"I'm just calling to say hi, really. But we *are* celebrating an anniversary soon, and I—"

"We are? What is it? Our—"

"Eric, I was kind of wondering if you had any special feelings about that time in your life, now that it's almost twelve years since we graduated. I mean . . . Well, I guess it might seem a little abrupt me calling you like this after all this time."

"It does a little bit."

"I've been thinking back on that time, and I was thinking about how innocent I was then, and I'm wondering what you remember about that time. Maybe you remember some things about me that you'd be willing to share."

"Ellie."

"Eric, the right thing to do, you know, generally, is to develop some kind of life outside the office, right? Don't you think? I have some things I like to do, you know, on weekends, but I haven't really been doing any of those things. It seems like I'm just always thinking about the problems at the office. It's kind of horrible. . . . Well, you know what? I don't want to talk about myself. I'd like to hear what you are doing. Are you still playing the viola?"

"Uh, actually, the viola is under the bed."

"Oh, that's too bad."

"Well . . ."

"But you're still trying to write music?"

"Not really. I guess I'm—"

"What *are* you doing, then?"

"I'm in pharmaceutical sales."

It hadn't occurred to her before that he could be some kind of Eric impostor. His voice was similar but maybe a little huskier and flatter, with fewer nasal resonances. The voice of Eric if he'd put on forty pounds. The thought disturbed her.

"Have you been smoking?"

"Not that I know of, Ellie."

"What does that mean?"

"It means I haven't been smoking at all. But why do you ask?"

"Your voice sounds different."

"Maybe when you haven't talked to someone in eleven or twelve years—"

"I'm going to ask you some questions that only Eric could answer, okay?"

"Ellie, are you—"

"What color was the sweater I bought you?"

"I don't remember any sweater that you bought me."

"That's correct. And what was my favorite brand of cigarettes?"

"Ellie, we're not going to do this."

"Eric, if we don't I'll start worrying."

"You're sounding a little distraught to me, Ellie."

"Cigarettes, Eric. Or I'm going to have to—"

If she were to remember the conversation in its best light, she would remember it ending with an effectively deployed feminine ultimatum. But in fact it didn't end as shown. What happened next was that her boyfriend from college, who no longer resembled the romantic violist of her recollection, interrupted her, began to lecture her—"Ellie, I'm a little concerned about the way you're talking right now"—commencing to give a long, not entirely related motivational speech about pharmaceutical sales, and how in pharmaceutical sales, when you were about to "close the deal" with the "mark," you had to read the client "just the right way." You had to look deep into her eyes, Eric said, to see the layers of frailty everywhere in her. This moist expression of frailty was where she was "unfinished," Eric observed, where she still needed something, where she still had some residual bit of longing that hadn't been wiped out. This was the point at which pharmaceutical sales became important, Eric said. "Ellie, I know I'm not doing what I thought I was going to do back then, and I know I'm not doing anything very memorable, but one thing I have learned how to do is read the client. I can tell you the truth about a person from twenty yards away. I can see the little things that are hidden." There was only this dollar-store world, with its petroleum-based geegaws, awaiting the flood, and in this world there was just Eric and his mark, the doctor or druggist who was going to realize that he really needed to prescribe or stockpile a virility drug or a treatment for male-pattern baldness, and he needed to do it *now*.

Ellie Knight-Cameron had now been awake many hours. This was the essence of being alive. She intended to investigate one last person, namely Maureen Jones, who was in charge of the mail room at K&K. The impartial observer might have imagined that the mail room was not an important division of the K&K organization. He or she might infer from Ellie's investigation that the mail room was somehow an afterthought in the important day-to-day activities of Kolodny & Kolodny. But this was incorrect. The mail room, which was not a room but a mail alcove, was where the contracts were sent out and where they were received, later to be signed and notarized by relevant parties. It also dispatched holiday cards and gifts.

Ellie catalogued the facts she knew about Maureen.

Maureen was the one and only African American employee of Kolodny & Kolodny.

Naturally, Ellie had been loath to conclude that Maureen was guilty of crimes relating to the suggestion box. She had avoided this supposition. Ellie had always imagined herself sensitive to the needs and wishes of people regardless of race, creed, or sexual orientation. In her elementary school, for example. There were some Native American children. She had this one friend, Deanna, a Native American girl. Her folks were poor, even by the standards of a hippie girl whose own parents barely worked. Ellie liked Deanna a lot. She was gentle. Deanna wore braids and big homely glasses. The one unusual thing about Deanna was that she never talked. Her parents rarely did either. Still, their friendship lasted for a time. Then, suddenly, it was the middle school years, and you know what happens then. A big wave comes and washes over the sun-dappled beach where all the kids are standing, and the kids are sucked into the sea, flung down into the murky backwash, upended, cast upon the rocks, battered, concussed. Some never emerge from the rip. Some are so badly shaken that they will never go near the water again. Some are proud, some are brought low, some forget everything that befell them. Of the vast majority of kids you know or love, you suddenly realize you know nothing at all. Now that these individuals have the ocean of hormones calling to them, lighting up their neglected circuitry so that their bodies look like the pink physiognomic overlays from old encyclopedias, *all is different*. Through the actions of this middle school tidal wave, completely different kids have been washed down to your section of the beach, with different needs and desperations, and you're stuck with them, at least until college.

To put it another way: Deanna, the Native American kid,

developed *other interests*. Her interests no longer included
Ellie Knight-Cameron, or Ellie Knight-Cameron's collection
of paper dolls, or Ellie's 45 rpm vinyl records of soft rock
favorites. This all became apparent one night with her at a
convenience store. At this store, which was more inconven-
ient than convenient, there were older boys and convertibles.
There was strategic shoplifting of slushies and pornography,
and some use of the word *pussy*.

Therefore, Maureen Jones needed to be dealt with thought-
fully. Maureen was stuck in an office full of older, bitchy
white ladies. Maureen had to drive all the way over from the
other side of town, from an area now ringed entirely by corporate headquarters in foul glass boxes, companies that had
abandoned New York City for the advantageous tax policies
of Connecticut. Maureen drove across this color barrier into
the suburban part of Stamford, where the white people were.
It was a trip Ellie now had to make in the reverse. And this
was how she came to be camped out in front of a modest
town house tucked in beside the projects. A stone's throw
from the homely Amtrak station, five minutes from the
backwash of Long Island Sound.

Having made it all the way here, having parked across
from the residence in question, Ellie found, however, that
she was unable to knock on the door. She was afraid to
knock; she was even afraid to get out of the car. She'd locked
all the doors. It was after midnight now, and tomorrow was
another workday. It would *not* be the right thing to do, to
wake Maureen Jones in order to make a citizen's arrest.
Well, maybe it *was* the right thing to do. Maybe the right
thing to do was to call the police and barge into the building, wake Maureen Jones, and then quickly get on a plane

back to Arizona, where her mother was to enter a halfway house.

Ellie had been staked out for a couple of hours, trying to vanish into her contoured driver's seat with meager lower-back support, when a sinister-looking man who probably wasn't sinister at all came walking along the avenue toward Maureen Jones's house. He was wearing clothes of astonishing bagginess. Everything about the bagginess of his outfit was meant to facilitate the concealment of contraband items. Or not. Ellie Knight-Cameron watched the man look both ways before crossing the street. He strode to the door of Jones's house, knocked, was admitted, and disappeared inside.

Ellie would grant that *one man*, even at this particularly late hour, was not a conspiracy. But this man was followed by another—a younger, shorter man who, when he was cascaded with the glare of streetlight, appeared to be sporting ornamental braids. This second man, whose garb was an athletic warm-up outfit, he too was admitted into Maureen Jones's residence. Not fifteen minutes passed before a third appeared, a grizzled older fellow with a mane of impressive dreadlocks. This man must have been an elder statesman of the movement. Although Ellie Knight-Cameron did not have night-vision goggles or any other sophisticated surveillance items, she believed nonetheless that she saw this third man make some kind of eccentric hand gesture that proved him worthy of admittance.

Finally, a woman was allowed into Jones's house. The situation was no different from those described above except that now a woman was involved. In no single case could Ellie see *who* was opening the door and admitting these strangers. Yet she could see that people were in fact entering the Jones residence. They would sidle up to the front door, knock once, perform the *jazz hands* gesture, the door would swing back, and the stranger would then slip into the house.

What exactly did Maureen Jones's organization believe in? Ellie reviewed. She paged through the suggestions in order. She had saved them, of course, and here they were, in her lap, like artifacts of antiquity:

(A) If they're going to close lanes on the parkway, they ought to actually repair the goddamned road. (B) You ought to throw this fucking coffee machine out the window and run over it with a car. (C) Worldwide revolution now. Throw off your chains. (D) All of you should be lined up and shot.

Considered in this way, there was a menacing progression to the Kolodny & Kolodny suggestions. In the first suggestion, the government was being called into question, the ability of the government to govern, to make decisions for the public good. In the second, the office itself was being castigated, as well as its daily diet of events: coffee breaks, luncheons, and so forth. In the third suggestion, Ellie thought, the conspiracy was calling upon the disgruntled populace to overthrow the existing order. And in the fourth, armed struggle began.

In the last moment before the necessity for action propelled her, Ellie had a disturbing thought. Wasn't it possible that a person or persons in the office was *colluding* with Maureen Jones? Why hadn't she considered it before? Any number of alliances could figure in this conspiratorial model, alliances comprised of employees present and past: Maureen and Angie, Maureen and Dolly, Maureen and Bonnie, Maureen and Astrid, Maureen and Neil Rubinstein, or even Maureen and Duane himself. Wasn't Duane's surname uncomfortably close to the world *collude?* And if two of the K&K family, why not three of them? What about Maureen and Angie and Dolly? Were there occasions when the three of them had appeared to be whispering conspiratorially? And if three, why not four? With four people, you know, they'd have a lock on office communications.

In the stillness of the street, Ellie felt flushed, confused, ashamed, abandoned by the commonplaces of the day. The reliable items of her adopted landscape, the material things before her—the sickly ginkgo trees of the block, stray cats, a rumbling garbage truck—were not as they appeared. There was a menace to objects and situations that were anything but menacing. She knew at once the likelihood of calamity, as would any good employee of K&K: great vengeful floods, tornadoes, explosions, acts of God. In the desert landscape of this Knight-Cameron fever, men and women lurched thirstily, disaffiliated from their inamoratas. She had never been as alone as this, as condemned. Maybe Eric was right, and she had not learned to *read the client,* the him or her who was *not* trying to take from Ellie what little she had, what modicum of serenity she had carved out for herself, thousands of miles from home. Maybe everyone was *not* trying to take her few possessions and run her out into the street; maybe every man she encountered was not trying to insult her person; maybe the bulk of those she encountered in the dark years of the war on terror were also innocents, people who were just trying to make an honest living and put by a little cash in case of dire accident. She blamed Duane and she blamed Chris Grady. Someone had to be blamed. Because injustice persisted well after the avengers of injustice were rendered impotent by exhaustion, scandal, prescription abuse, and appearances on the talk-show circuit.

In the end, it was this notion of injustice that enabled her to climb from her Dodge Omni. Injustice, and impatience, and a self-destructive need to finish a project even if it was a bad idea. She reeled onto the streets of Stamford, blushing horribly, knees weak, to charge with malicious crimes those persons who would threaten her peaceable office life. Those who would oppress the wage-earners of the new world order. Into the light weaved Ellie Knight-Cameron, lover of minor league baseball and the tango, delusional thinker, energetic misreader of signs and symbols, bound to collide, if not collude, with the mystery of all mysteries, which is the total absence of mystery in a market economy.

In due course, despite misgivings, she reached the front door of the Jones residence. And having girded herself, she was ready to knock. It was some kind of cheap hollow-core door, the sort you expect from a bankrupt home renovation chain, or from a stage set. Ellie Knight-Cameron knocked on it with the force of a patriot.

Merriment was taking place inside. She could hear merriment within. Was it possible that people could find pleasure in causing others hurt and dismay? Because Ellie *was* hurt and dismayed, and she intended to get satisfaction. It was as if they were laughing about it all. Ellie knocked again, and she heard the giddy excitement in the room diminish for a moment.

Would she be able to go through with it? Would she be able to face with equanimity the perils of revelation? Would there be guns? Should she call the authorities? Before she could change her mind, which she was dying to do, the door swung back, and there was a cry, an éclat, and the cry was enormous, enough to trouble the curtains nearby, up and down the block. And the cry was the word *SURPRISE!* "Surprise!" they called. "Surprise! *Surprise!*"

The inside of the Jones residence, she saw, was modest, as modest as the exterior, and it was neatly appointed, and there were streamers leading from the tops of the lamp shades to the curtain rods above, and then again from one of the chairs all the way over to the windowsill, and there was a little dog, a yapper, and even the dog had a ribbon around its neck, and there were some children, toddlers, wearing conical hats, and there were a lot of black faces, African American faces, and all of these faces had evidently been enjoying themselves or at least they were enjoying themselves until they got a good look at Ellie Knight-Cameron. Then something imperceptible vanished from their expressions. Because Ellie Knight-Cameron was *not* who they thought would be coming through the door when they shouted *surprise*.

"Can we help you?" said the woman holding open the door.

"I'm looking for Maureen Jones," Ellie said.

"She's not here."

"I'm betting she *is* there." Only slowly did the horrible truth dawn in Ellie Knight-Cameron. It worked its way up her esophagus. The revelation.

"Who are you?" the woman said.

"I work with Maureen."

"Well, if you work with her, then you know she's still at work."

"I don't know any such thing, because I saw her leave work this afternoon, early, along with everyone else."

"She's still *at* work."

"I don't think I believe you!"

This argument might have continued escalating, had not Maureen herself happened upon the scene. Yes, Maureen Jones was soon present. As the above exchange was taking place, Maureen was in the midst of yanking her purse out of the passenger seat, locking the car door, and taking her sweet time. Maureen was coming up the street. What she was coming up the street *in* was a uniform, and the uniform was of her second job, her night shift, where two nights a week she worked as a cashier at a certain fast-food enterprise. And the color of the uniform was teal, and the function of the uniform was to render Maureen Jones selfless, indistinguishable, objectified. Before the situation between Ellie and the woman at the door of Maureen's house had been resolved, Maureen herself did have the opportunity to mediate, just as the cry of *Surprise* was altered and became instead the cry of *Happy birthday! Happy birthday, Maureen!*

Maureen began laughing in an easygoing and careless way that was impossible not to see as beautiful, even moving, because Maureen, despite the fact that she didn't smile easily, had a sweet smile, at least until Maureen realized that Ellie Knight-Cameron from K&K, her grim day job, was standing on her doorstep at some forbidding hour of the morning. Ellie Knight-Cameron was meanwhile apprehending the facts, namely that she, Maureen Jones, mother of two, was working two jobs, and Maureen was somewhat unhappy that this bit of information was now in wider distribution. But before Ellie could say anything, before she could defend herself about turning up on the doorstep of Maureen Jones's residence, before Ellie could say anything about it, Maureen was inviting her inside. And so the conclusion was delayed.

Which conclusion? The one in which Ellie was herself the only possible author of the suggestions? And if she was the only person who could have failed to see this, if it was evident to even the most casual observer that she was both protagonist and antagonist, what did this tell us about the way we lived in those days?

III

The Albertine Notes

The first time I got high all I did was make sure these notes came out all right. I mean, I wanted the girl at the magazine to offer me work again, and that was going to happen only if the story sparkled. There wasn't much work then because of the explosion. The girl at the magazine was saying, "Look, you don't have to *like* the assignment, just *do* the assignment. If you don't want it, there are people lined up behind you." And she wasn't kidding. There really were people lined up. Out in reception. An AI receptionist, in a makeshift lobby, in a building on Staten Island, the least affected precinct of the beleaguered City of New York. Writers spilling into the foyer, shouting at the robot receptionist. All eager to show off their clips.

The editor was called Tara. She had turquoise hair. She looked like a girl I knew when I was younger. Where was that girl now? Back in the go-go days you could yell a name at the TV and it would run a search on the identities associated with that name. For a price. Credit card records, toll plaza visits, loan statements, *you set the parameters*. My particular Web video receiver, in fact, had a little pop-up window in the corner of the image that said, *Want to see what your wife is doing right now?* Was I a likely customer for this kind of snooping based on past purchases? Anyway, recreational detection and character assassination, that was all *before* Albertine.

Street name for the buzz of a lifetime. Bitch goddess of the overwhelming past. Albertine. Rapids in the river of time. Take just a little into your bloodstream and any memory you've ever had is available to you all over again. That and more. Not a memory like you've experienced it before, not a little tremor in some *presque vu* register of your helter-skelter consciousness: *Oh yeah, I remember when I ate peanut butter and jelly with Serena on Boston Common and drank rum out of paper cups.* No, the actual event itself, completely renewed, playing in front of you as though you were experiencing it for the first time. There's Serena in blue jeans with patches on the knees, the green Dartmouth sweatshirt that goes with her eyes, drinking the rum a little too fast and spitting out some of it, picking her teeth with her deep red nails, a shade called *lycanthrope*, and there's the taste of super-chunky peanut butter in the sandwiches, stale pretzel rods. Here you are, the two of you, walking around that part of the garden with all those willows. She lets slip your hand because your palms are moist: the smell of a city park at the moment when a September shower dampens the pavement, car exhaust, a mist hanging in the air at dusk, the sound of kids fighting over the rules of softball, a homeless dude scamming you for a sip of your rum.

Get the idea?

It almost goes without saying that Albertine appeared in a certain socioeconomic sector not long *after the blast*. When you're used to living a comfortable middle-class life, when you're used to going to the organic farmers' market on the weekend, maybe a couple of dinners out at that new Indian place, you're bound to become *very uncomfortable* when fifty square blocks of your city suddenly look like a NASA photo of Mars. You're bound to look for some relief when you're camped in a school gymnasium pouring condensed milk over government-issued cornflakes. Under the circumstances, you're going to prize your memories, right? So you'll skin-pop some Albertine, or you'll use the eyedropper, hold open your lid, and go searching back through the halcyon days. Afternoons in the stadium, those stadium lights on the grass, the first roar of the crowd. Or how about your first concert? Or your first kiss?

Only going to cost you twenty-five bucks.

I'm Kevin Lee. Chinese American, third generation, which doesn't mean my dad worked in a delicatessen to get me into MIT. It means my father was an IT venture capitalist and my mother was a microbiologist. I grew up in Newton, Mass., but I also lived in northern California for a while. I came to New York City to go to Fordham, dropped out, and started writing about the sciences for one of the alternative weeklies. It was a start. But the offices of the newspaper, all of its owners, a large percentage of its shareholders, and nine-tenths of its reporting staff were incinerated. Not like I need to bring all of that up again. If you want to assume anything, assume that all silences from now on have some grief in them.

One problem with Albertine was that the memories she screened were not all good, naturally. Albertine didn't guarantee good memories. In fact, Albertine guaranteed at least a portion of pretty awful memories. One guy I interviewed, early on when I was chasing the story, he spoke about having only memories about jealousy. He got a bad batch, probably too many additives, and all he could see in his mind's eye were these intense moments of jealousy. He was even weeping when we spoke. On the come down. I'd taken him out to an all-night diner. Where Atlantic Avenue meets up with Conduit. Know that part of the city? A beautiful, a neglected part. Ought to have been a chill in the early-autumn night. Air force jets were landing at the airport in those days. The guy, we'll say his name is Bob, he was telling me about the morning he called a friend, Nina, to meet her for a business breakfast. In the middle of the call Nina told him that his wife, Maura, had become her lover. He remembered everything about this call, the exact wording of the revelation. *Bob, Maura has been attracted to me since as far back as your wedding.* He remembered the excruciating pauses. He could overhear the rustling of bedclothes. All these things he could picture, just as though they were happening, and even the things he *imagined* during the phone call, which took place seventeen years ago. What Nina had done to Maura in bed, what dildo they used. It was seventeen years later on Atlantic and Conduit, and Maura had been vaporized, or that's what Bob said: "Jesus, Maura is dead and I never told her what was great about our years together, and I'll never have that chance now." He was inconsolable, but I kept asking questions. Because I'm a reporter. I put it together that he'd spent fifty bucks on two doses of Albertine. Six months after the thyroid removal, here he was. Bob was just hoping to have one sugary memory—of swimming in the pond in Danbury, the swimming hole with the rope swing. Remember that day? And all he could remember was that his wife had slept with his college friend, and that his brother took the girl he dreamed about in high school. Like jealousy was the only color in his life. Like the atmosphere was three parts jealousy, one part oxygen.

That's what Albertine was whispering in his ear.

Large-scale drug dealing, it's sort of like beta testing. There are unscrupulous people around. Nobody knows how a chemical is going to behave until the guinea pigs have lined up. FDA thinks they know, when they rubber-stamp some compound that makes you grow back the hair you lost during chemotherapy. But they know nothing. Try giving your drug to a hundred and fifty thousand disenfranchised members of the new middle-class poor in a recently devastated American city. Do it every day for almost a year. Allow people to mix in randomly their favorite inert substances.

There were lots of stories. Lots of different experiences. Lots of fibs, exaggerations, innuendos, rumors. Example: not only did Albertine cause bad memories as frequently as good memories—this was the lore—but she also allowed you to *remember the future*. This is what Tara told me when she assigned me the 2,500 words. "Find out if it's true. Find out if we can get to the future on it."

"What would *you* do with it?"

"None of your business," she said, and then, like she was covering her tracks, "I'd see if I was ever going to get a promotion."

Well, here's another example. The story of Deanna, whose name I'm changing for her protection: "I was going to church after the blast, you know, because I was kind of feeling like God should be doing something about all the heartache. I mean, maybe that's simpleminded or something. I don't care. I was in church, and it was a beautiful place; any church still standing was a beautiful place when you had those horrible clouds overhead all the time and everybody getting sick. The fact of the matter is, while I was there in church, during what should have been a really calm time, instead of thinking that the Gospels were good news, I was having a *vision*. I don't know what else to call it. It was like in the movies, when the movie goes into some kind of flashback, except in this vision I saw myself driving home from church, and I saw a car pulling ahead of me out onto the road by the reservoir, and I had this feeling that the car pulling out toward the reservoir, which was a twenty-year-old model of one of those minivans, was some kind of bad omen, you know? So I went to my priest and I told him what I thought, that this car had some bad intention, at least in my mind's eye, you know. I could see it; I could see that Jesus was telling me this, better watch out at the reservoir. Some potion was going to be emptied into the reservoir. I could see it, *I have seen it.* The guys doing it, they were emptying jugs in and they definitely had mustaches. They were probably from some desert country. The priest took me to the bishop, and I repeated everything I knew, about the Lord and what he had told me, and so I had an audience with the archbishop. The archbishop said, 'You have to tell me if Jesus really told you this. Did Jesus tell you *personally?* Is this a genuine message from *the Christ?*' In this office with a lot of dusty books on the dusty shelves. You could tell that they were all really hungry to be in the room with the word of *the Christ*, and who wouldn't feel that way? Everybody is desperate, right? But then one of them says, 'Roll up your sleeves, please.'"

Deanna was shown the door. Because of the needle tracks. Now she's working down by the Gowanus Expressway.

The archbishop did give the tip to the authorities, however, just to be on the safe side, and the authorities *did* stop a Ford Explorer on the way to the reservoir in Katonah. And Deanna's story was just one along these lines. Many Albertine users began reporting "memories" of things that were yet to happen. Outcomes of elections, declines in various international stocks, the intensity of the upcoming hurricane season. The dealers, whether skeptical or believing on this point, saw big profits in mythology. Because garbage heads and gamblers often live right next door to one another, know what I mean? One vice is like another. Soon there were those scraggly guys that you used to see at the track. These guys were all looking to cop Albertine from the man in Red Hook or East New York, and they were sitting like autistics in a room with Sheetrock torn from the walls, no electricity, no running water, people pissing themselves, refusing food, and they were in search of the name of the greyhound that was going to take the next race. Maybe they could bet the trifecta? Teeth were falling out of the heads of these bettors, and their hair was falling out, because they believed if they just hung on long enough, they would get the vision.

Now, that's marketing.

Logically speaking, there were some issues with a belief system like this. On Albertine, the visions of the past were mixed up with the alleged future, of course. And sometimes these were nightmarish visions. You had to know where to cast your gaze. There was no particular targeting of receptors. The drug wasn't advanced. It was like using a lawnmower to harvest wildflowers. I shook one girl awake, Cassandra, down in the Hot Zone in Bed-Stuy. I knew Cassandra was a bullshit name, the kind of name you'd tell a reporter. It was a still night, coming on toward December, bitter cold, because the debris cloud had really fucked with global warming, and I was walking around dictating into a digital recorder, okay? The streets were uninhabited. I mean, take a city from eight million down to four and a half million, suddenly everything seems kind of *empty*. And this is a pedestrian town anyhow. Now more than ever. I was on my way to interview an epidemiologist who claimed that while on Albertine he'd had a *memory* of the proper way to eradicate the drug. He'd tell me only if I would remunerate him. And maybe Tara would reimburse me, because I had run through most of the few hundred dollars I had in cash before my bank was wiped off the map. I'd already sold blood and volunteered for a dream lab.

But on the way to the epidemiologist, I saw this girl nodding out on a swing, an old wooden swing, the kind that usually gets stolen in the projects. Over by a middle school in the Hot Zone. I picked up her arm; she didn't even seem to notice at first. I turned it over. Like I couldn't tell from the rings under the eyes, those black bruises that said, *This one has remembered too much.* I checked her arms anyway. Covered with lesions.

I said, "Hey, I'm doing a story for one of those *tits and lit* mags. About Albertine. Wondering if I can ask you a few questions."

Her voice was frail at first, almost as if it were the first voice ever used:

"Ask me any question. I'm like the oracle at Delphi, boy-friend."

Sort of a dark-haired girl, and she sort of reminded me of Serena. Wearing this red scarf on her head. A surge from her voice, like I'd heard it before, like maybe I was almost verging on something from the past. I figured I'd try out Cassandra, see what kind of a fact-gathering resource she could be, see where it led. It beat watching the Hasidim in Crown Heights fighting with the West Indians. Man, I'd had enough with the Hasidim and the Baptists and their rants about *end-times*. The problem was that Albertine, bitch goddess, kept giving conflicting reports about which end-times we were going to get.

"What's my name?" I asked.

"Your name is Kevin Lee. You're from Massachusetts."

"Okay, uh, what am I writing about?"

"You're writing about Albertine, and you're in way over your head. And the batteries on your recording device are going to run out soon."

"Thanks for the tip. Are we going to kiss?"

A reality-testing question, get it?

No inflection at all, Cassandra said: "Sure. We are. But not now. *Later.*"

"What do you know about the origins of Albertine?"

"What do you want to know?"

"Are you high now?"

Which was like asking if she'd ever seen rain.

"Are you high enough to see the origins from where you are sitting?"

"I'd have to be there to have a memory of it."

"What have you heard?" I asked.

"Everybody's heard *something*."

"I haven't."

"You aren't listening. Everybody knows."

"Then tell me," I said.

"You have to be inside. Take the drug, then you'll be inside."

Up at the corner, a blue-and-white sedan—NYPD—as rare as a white tiger in this neighborhood. The police were advance men for the drug cartels. They had no peacetime responsibility, except they made sure that the trade proceeded without any interference. For this New York's Finest got a cut, a portion of which they tithed back to the city. So the syndicate was subsidizing the City of New York, the way I saw it. Subsidizing the rebuilding, subsidizing the government, so that government would have buildings, underground bunkers, treatment centers, whole departments devoted to Albertine, to her care and protection.

Fox, a small-time dealer and friend of Bob, one of my sources, was the first person I could find who'd float these conspiratorial theories. Right before he disappeared. And he wasn't the only one who disappeared among the people I came to know. Bob stopped returning my calls too. Not that it amounted to much, a disappearance here and there. Our city was outside of history now, beyond surveillance. People disappeared.

"I don't, like, buy the conspiracy angle," I said to Cassandra. "Been there, done that."

Her eyes fluttered, as if she were fighting off an invasion of butterflies.

"Well, actually . . . ," she said.

"Government isn't competent enough for conspiracy. Government is a bunch of guys in a subbasement somewhere in Englewood, waiting for some war to blow over. Guys hoping they won't have to see what everyone out on the street has seen."

I helped her from the swing. She was thin, like a greyhound, and just as distracted. The chains on the swing clattered as she dismounted.

It wasn't that hard to be at the center of the Albertine story, see, because there was no center. Everywhere, people were either selling the drug or using the drug, and if they were using the drug, they were in its thrall, which was the thrall of memory. You could see them lying around everywhere. In all public places. Albertine expanded to fill any container. If you thought she was confined to Red Hook, it seemed for a while that she was only in Red Hook. But then if you looked in Astoria, she was in Astoria too. As if it were the act of observing that somehow turned her up. More you looked, more you saw. A city whose citizens, when outdoors, seemed preoccupied or vacant. If inside, almost paralytic. I couldn't tell you how many times in that first week of reporting I happened to gaze into a ground-floor window and see people staring at television screens that were turned *off*.

So I went on with the theories:

"People think the government has the juice to launch conspiracies. But if they were competent enough for that kind of subterfuge, then they'd be competent enough to track some guy who brings a suitcase detonator into the country across the Canadian border and has the uranium delivered to him by messenger. Some messenger on a bike! They'd be competent enough to prevent a third of Manhattan getting blown up! Or they'd be able to infiltrate the cartels. Or they'd be able to repair all of this civic destruction. So are we going to kiss now?"

"Later," she said.

I was thinking that maybe this conversation had come to an end, that there was no important subtext to the conversation, that Cassandra was just another deep-fried intelligence locked away in the past, and that maybe I should have gone on my way to pay off the epidemiologist who had the new angle. But then she *was* sneaking me a little bit of insider information; she said, "Brookhaven."

Meaning what? Meaning the laboratory?

Of course, the Brookhaven theory, like the MIT theory, like the Palo Alto Research Center theory or the Jet Propulsion Lab theory. These rumors about Albertine just weren't all that compelling, because everyone had heard them, but for some reason I had this uncanny sense of recognition at the name of the government facility on Long Island. Then she said that we should together *go see the man.*

"I don't know exactly about the beginning, the origin," Cassandra said, "but I've been with someone who does. He'll be there. Where we're going."

"What are you seeing right now?"

"Autumn," she whispered.

It was a coming-down thing. The imagery of Albertine began to move toward the ephemeral, the passing away, leaves mulching, pumpkin seeds, first frost. Was there some neurotransmitter designated as the seat of memory that necessarily had autumn written into it? A chromosome that contained a sensitivity to fall? When I was a kid there were a couple years we lived in northern California, a charmed place, you know, during the tech boom. Those words seem quaint. Like saying *whore with a heart of gold*. I couldn't forget northern California, couldn't forget the redwoods, the seals, the rugged beaches, the austere Pacific, and when I heard the words *tech boom*, I knew what memory I would have if I took the drug, which was the memory of the first autumn that I didn't get to see the seasons change. In northern California, watching the mist creep into the bay, watching the Golden Gate engulfed, watching that city disappear. In northern California, I waited till evening, then I'd go over to the used-book stores in town, because there was always someone in the used-book stores who was from Back East. So this would be my memory, a memory of reading, of stealing time from time itself, of years passing while I was reading, hanging out in a patched armchair in a used-book store in northern California and, later on, back in Mass. Maybe I was remembering this memory or maybe I was constructing it.

We were going over the bridge, the Kosciusko, where there was only foot traffic these days. Down Metropolitan Ave., from Queens to Brooklyn, over by where the tanks used to be. Not far from the cemetery. You know what you might have seen there, right? Used to be the skyline; you used to see it there every day, caught in traffic, listening to the all-news format. Maybe you got bored of the skyline rising above you, maybe it was like a movie backdrop, there it was again; you'd seen it so many times that it meant nothing, skyscrapers like teeth on the insipid grin of enterprise, cemetery and skyscrapers, nice combination. The greatest city in the world? Once my city was the greatest, but this was *not* the view anymore, on the night that I walked across the bridge with Cassandra. No more view, right? Because there were the debris clouds, and there was the caustic rain that fell on all the neighborhoods, a rain that made everybody sick afterward, a rain that made people choke and puke. People wore gas masks on the Kosciusko. Gas masks were *the* cut-rate fashion statement. South of Citicorp Center, whose tampon applicator summit had been blown clean off, there was *nothing*. Get it? You could see all the way to Jersey during the day. If the wind was blowing right. Edgewater. You could see the occasional lights of Edgewater, NJ. There was no Manhattan to see, and there was no electricity in Manhattan where the buildings remained. The generator plant downtown had been obliterated. Emergency lights, not much else.

People just turned their backs on Manhattan. They forgot about that island, which was the center of nothing, except maybe the center of society ladies with radiation burns crowding the trauma units at the remaining hospitals. Manhattan was just landfill now. And there are no surprises in a landfill. Unless you're a seagull.

Outer boroughs, that was where the action was. Like this place where we were going. It'd been a smelting plant, and the police cars were lined up around it; the cops were all around it like they were the blue border of imagination. It was a ghost factory, and I dictated these impressions because the digital recorder was still recording. When I played back my notes, there was a section of the playback that was nothing but a sequence of words about autumn: *soaping windows, World Series, school supplies, yellow jackets, presidential elections, hurricane season.* Who was I trying to kid? I was *pretending* I was writing a story about Albertine. I was writing nothing.

Cassandra was mumbling: "They were fine-tuning some interrogation aids, or they had made a chemical error with some antidepressants or with ECT technologies, or they saw it in the movies and just duplicated the effects. They figured out how to do it with electrodes, or they figured out how to prompt certain kinds of memories, and then they thought perhaps they could coerce certain kinds of testimony with electrodes. They could torture certain foreign nationals, force confessions from these people, and the confessions would be freely signed because the memories would be *true*. Who's going to argue with a memory?"

"How do you know all of this?"

We stood in front of a loading-dock elevator, and the cops were frozen around us, hands on holsters—cops out front, nervous cops, cops waiting on the loading dock, cops everywhere—and the shadows in the elevator shaft danced because the elevator was *coming for us*. The elevator was the only light.

"I can see," Cassandra said.

"In the big sense?"

The only time she smiled in the brief period I knew her, when I was up close enough to see her lesions. People were so busy firing chemicals into their bodies, so busy trying to live in the past, that their cancers were blossoming. Or they stopped worrying about whether the syringe was dirty. And they stopped going to the clinics or the emergency rooms.

They let themselves vanish out of the world, as if by doing so they could get closer to some point of origin: your mom on your fourth birthday, smiling, holding out her hands, *Darling, it's your birthday!*

She said, "Think biochemistry," and she had the eye-dropper out again. "Think quantum mechanics. What would happen if you could harness some of the electrical charges in the brain by bombarding it with certain kinds of free particles?"

Her eyes were hopelessly bloodshot. She had a mean case of pinkeye. And her pupils were dilated.

"And because it's all about electrical charges, it's all about power, right? And about who has the power."

I was holding her hand, don't know why. Trying to stop her from dribbling more of that shit into her eye. I wasn't under any particular illusion about what was happening. I was lonely. Why hadn't I gone back up to Massachusetts? Why hadn't I called my cousins across town to see if they were okay? I was hustling. I knew things, but I didn't know when to stop researching and when to get down to work. There was always another trapdoor in the history of Albertine, another theory to chase down, some epidemiologist with a new slant. Some street addict who would tell you things, if you paid.

I knew, for example, that a certain Eduardo Cortez had consolidated himself as a kingpin of the Albertine trade, at least in Manhattan and Brooklyn, and that he occasionally drove his confederates around in military convoy. Everyone claimed to have seen the convoy, Jeeps and Hummers. Certain other dealers in the affected neighborhoods, like

Mnemonic X in Fort Greene, the 911 Gang in Long Island City, a bunch of them had been *neutralized*, as the language goes. I knew all of this, and still I walked into the ghost factory in Greenpoint like I was somebody, not an Asian kid sent by a soft-core porn mag, who rode up in the elevator with a girl whose skin looked like a relief map, a prostitute in a neighborhood where almost everyone was a prostitute. As Fox, Bob's dealer, told me before he disappeared, *You'd be amazed what a woman will do for a dealer.*

"When Cortez tied off, you know, everything changed," Cassandra said. It was one of those elevators that took forever. She'd been thinking what I was thinking before I even got to saying it. Her lips were cracked; her teeth were bad. She had once been brilliant, I could tell, or maybe that's just how I wanted it to be. Maybe she'd been brilliant; maybe she'd been at a university once. But now we used different words of praise for those we admired: *shrewd, tough.* And the most elevated term of respect: *alive.* Cortez was Dominican, *alive*, and thus he was part of the foul-is-fair demographics of Albertine. He was *from nowhere*, raised up in a badly depressed economy. Cortez had been a bike messenger and then a delivery truck driver, and some of his associates insisted that his business was still about message delivery. *We just trying to run a business.*

I'd seen the very site of Cortez's modest childhood and current residence recently; took me almost ten hours to get there, which tells you nothing. It's a big mistake to measure space in time, after all. Because times change. Still, Cortez had the longest subway ride of anyone in the drug trade. If he wanted to go look after his operatives in

Brooklyn, he had to get all the way from northern Manhattan to Brooklyn, and most of those lines didn't run anymore. Under the circumstances, a military convoy was just a good investment.

Washington Heights. Up north. Kids playing stickball in the street using old-fashioned boom microphones for bats. There were gangsters with earpieces on stoops up and down the block. What were the memories of these people like? Did they *drop*, as the addicts put it? Did they use? And what were Cortez's memories like? Memories of middleweight prizefighting at the gym up the block? Maybe. Some drinking with the boys. Some whoring around with the streetwalkers on Upper Broadway. Assignations with Catholic girls in the neighborhood? Cortez had a bad speech impediment, everybody said. Would Albertine make it so that he, in memory, could get as far back as the time *before* speech acquisition, to the sweet days before the neighborhood kids made fun of him for the way he talked? Could he teach his earlier self better how to say the *s* of American English? To speak with authority? One tipster provided by my magazine had offered sinister opinions about the appearance of Cortez, this Cortez of the assumed name. This tipster, whispering into a rare land line, had offered the theory that the culture of Albertine itself changed when Cortez appeared, just as did the culture of the continent when the original Cortez, great explorer, bearer of a shipload of smallpox, arrived. This was, of course, a variation on the so-called *diachronous theory of abuse patterns* that had turned up in the medical journals recently.

There were traditional kinds of memories before the appearance of Albertine, namely *identity builders*, according to these medical theorists. Like that guy at Brooklyn College, the government anthropologist of Albertine, Ernst Wentworth, PhD. Even repressed memory syndrome, in his way of thinking, is an *identity builder*, because in repressed memory syndrome you learn ultimately to *empower* yourself, in that you are identifying past abusers and understanding the ramifications of their misdeeds. *Empowerment* is the kind of terminology Wentworth used. A repetition of stressful memories is, according to his writing, an attempt by an identity to arrive at a solution to stress. Even a calamity, the collapse of a bridge, when remembered by one who has plunged into an icy river, is an *identity builder*, in that it reassures the remembering subject. The here and now puts him in the position of being *alive* all over again, no matter how painful it is to be alive. The Wentworth identity-building theory was the prevailing theory of memory studies, up until Albertine.

Since Albertine arrived on the scene after the blast, theorists eventually needed to consider the blast in all early Albertine phenomena. Figures, right? One night I felt that I'd started to understand these theories in a dramatic way, in my heart, or what was left of it, instead of in my head. I was at the armory, where I slept in a *closet*, really—used to be a supply closet, and there were still some supplies in there, some rug-cleaning solvents, some spot removers, extra towels. You never know when you might need this stuff. Anyway, the halls outside the supply closet echoed; you could hear every whisper in the halls of the armory, formerly an area for the storage of munitions. You could hear people coming and going. It wasn't and isn't a great place to live, when you consider that I used to have a studio in the

East Village. But compared to living in the great hall itself, where mostly people tried to erect cubicles for themselves, cubicles made out of cardboard or canvas or Sheetrock, the supply closet was not so bad. The privilege of doling out closets had fallen to an Albertine addict called Bertrand, and when I fixed up Bertrand with Fox and a few other dealers, I got bumped up to the supply closet right away. Any moths came after my remaining shirts and sweaters, I had all the insecticide I'd need.

This night I'm describing, I had a breakthrough of dialectical reasoning: I was hearing the *blast*. You know the conventional wisdom about combat veterans, loud noises suggesting the sharp crack of submachine gun fire, all that? I thought just the opposite. That certain *silences* re-created the blast, because there's something about fission, you know, it's soundless in a way, it suggests soundlessness, it's a violence contained in the opposite of violence, big effects from preposterously small changes. Say you were one of the four million who survived, you were far enough away that the *blast, heat, and radiation* could do their damage before the sound reached you, wherever you were. So it follows that the sound of the explosion would be best summoned up in *no sound at all*. The pauses in the haggard steps of the insomniacs of the armory walking past the door to my closet, this sound was the structured absence in what all our memories were seeking to suppress or otherwise avoid: the truth of the blast.

I'm not a philosopher. But my guess was that eventually people would start *remembering* the blast. You know? How could it be otherwise? I'm not saying I'm the person who came up with the idea; maybe the government mole did.

Maybe Ernst Wentworth did. I'm saying, I guess, that all memories verged on being memories of the blast, like footsteps in the echoing corridor outside my supply closet. Memories were like downpours of black raindrops. All noises were examples of the possibility of the noise of the blast, which was the limit of all possibilities of sound, and thus a limit on all possibilities of memory. For a lot of people, the blast was so traumatic they couldn't even remember where they were at the time, and I'm one of those people, I'm afraid, in case you were wondering. I know I was heading out to Jersey for a software convention in the New Brunswick area. At least, that's what I think I was doing. But I don't know how I got back. When I came to, Manhattan was gone.

People began to have memories of the blast while high. And people began to *die* of certain memories on the drug. Makes perfect sense. And this is part of the *diachronous theory of abuse patterns* that I was talking about before. First, Conrad Dixon, a former academic himself, was found dead in his apartment in the Flatbush section of Brooklyn, no visible sign of death, except that he'd just been seen scamming a bunch of dealers in Crown Heights. Was the death by reason of poisonous additives in the drug cocktail? That'd be a pretty good theory if he were the only person who died this way, but all at once *a lot* of people started dying, and it was my contention, anyhow, that they were *remembering the blast*. There were the bad memories in an ordinary fit of Albertine remembering, and then there was the memory of this moment of all moments, a sense of the number of people eliminated in the carnage, a sense of the kind of motive of the guy or guys, men or women, who managed to smuggle the dirty uranium device into town and then have it delivered, et cetera. An innocent thing when Conrad Dixon, or the others like him, first did what they did. In the early curve of the epidemic, everybody used Albertine alone because memories are most often experienced alone. And the recitation of them, well, it was just pretty dull: *Oh, let me tell you about the time I was in Los Angeles and I saw such and such a starlet at the table next to me, or about the time I broke my arm trying to white-water raft.* Or whatever your pathetic memory is. It's all the same, the brimming eyes of your daughter when she was a toddler and fell and got a bump on her head, I don't give a fuck, because I know what happened with Conrad Dixon, which is that he put the needle in his arm and then he was back in Midtown and looking down at the lower part of the island where he had spent his entire youth. A good thing, sure, that Conrad, that day, had to take that programmer's certification test up at Columbia, because instead of becoming a faint shadow on the side of some building on Union Square, he could see the entire neighborhood that he had worked in subsumed into *perfect light*, and he could feel the nausea rising in him, and he could see the cloud's outstretched arms, and all the information in him was wiped aside, he was a vacuum of facts, a memory vacuum, and again and again he could see the light, feel the incineration, and he knew something about radiation that he hadn't known before, about the surface of the stars. He knew that he was sick, knew that again he was going to have to live through the first few days, when everyone was suffering, their insides liquefying. Don't make me walk you through it—the point is that Albertine gave *back* the blast, when Conrad had hoped never to expe-

rience it again. Conrad was so stuck in the loop of this recollection that he could do nothing else but die, because that
was the end of the blast—whether in actual space or on the
recollected plane, whether in the past or the present or the
future, whether in ideas or reality—the blast was about
death.

What's this have to do with Eduardo Cortez? Well, it has
to do with the fact that Cortez's play for control of the Albertine cartel came exactly at the moment of highest density
of deaths from Albertine overdose or drug interaction. I refer you back again to the *diachronous theory of abuse patterns*.
See what I mean? The big question is how did Cortez, just
by showing up, affect the way Albertine was used? The mix-
ture of the chemical, if it's even a chemical, certainly didn't
change all that much—had not changed during the course
of the twelve months that it grew into a street epidemic. Can
we attribute the differences in abuse patterns to any other
factors? Why is it Cortez who seemed to be responsible for
the blast's intruding into everybody's memory?

My notes for the magazine are all about my disbelief, my
uncertainty. But I was holding Cassandra's hand, prostitute
in rags, woman with the skeletal body, while she was using
the eyedropper, and I know this might seem like a hopeful
gesture. Like some good could come of it all. I heard her
sigh. The cage of the elevator, at a crawl, passed a red emergency light on the wall of the shaft. Hookers are always
erotic about nonerotic things. Time, for example. The elsewhere of time was all over her, like she was coming to
memories of a time before prostitution, and this was somehow really alluring. I was holding her hand. I was disoriented.
I checked my watch. I mean I checked what day it was. I

had been assigned to the Albertine story two weeks ago, according to my Rolex knockoff—which had miraculously survived the electromagnetic pulse—but I could swear that it had been just *two days before* that I'd been hanging out in the offices of the soft-core porn mag, the offices with the bulletproof glass and the robot receptionist out front. When had I last been back to the supply closet to sleep? When had I last eaten? Wasn't it the night just passed, the evening with the footsteps in the corridor and the revelation about the silence of the blast? I was holding Cassandra's hand because she had a tenuous link to the facts of Albertine and this seemed like the last chance to *master* the story, to get it down somehow, instead of being consumed by it.

This is my scoop, then. The scoop is that suddenly I saw what she was seeing.

Cassandra said, "Watch this."

Pay close attention. I saw a close-up, *in my head I saw it,* like from some Web movie—a guy's arm, a man's arm, an arm covered with scars, almost furry it was so hairy, and then a hand pulling tight a belt around a biceps, jamming in a needle, depressing the plunger, a grunt of initial discomfort. Then the voice of the guy, thick accent, maybe a Dominican accent, announcing his threat: "I'm going back to the Lower East Side and I'm going to cap the motherfucker, see if I don't." Definite speech impediment. A problem with sibilance. You know? Then this guy, this dude, was looking over at Cassandra—she was in the scene, not in the elevator, where we were at least theoretically standing, but with Eduardo Cortez. She was his consort. He was taking her hand, there was a connection of hands, a circular movement of hands, and then Cassandra and I were on a street, and I saw Cortez in Tompkins Square Park, which doesn't exist anymore, of course, and it was clear that he was searching out a particular white guy, and now, coming through the crowd, here was the guy, looked like an educated man, if you know what I mean, one of those East Village art-slumming dudes. Cortez was searching out this guy, who was kinda grungy, wearing black jeans and a T-shirt, and it was all preordained, and now Cortez had found him.

Lights associated with the thrall of Cassandra's recollection, phantom lights, auras. The particulars were like a migraine. Things were solarized; there were solar flares around the street lamps. We were bustling in and around the homeless army of Tompkins Square. I could hear my own panicky breathing. I was in a park that didn't exist anymore, and I was seeing Cortez, and I was seeing this guy, this white guy—he had that look where one side of his face, the right side, was different from the other side, so that on the right side he seemed to be melancholy and placid, whereas on the left there was the faintest resemblance to a smirk at all times. The left side was all contorted, and maybe there were scars there, some kind of slasher's jagged line running from the corner of his mouth to his ear, and Cassandra, I guess, was saying, "Let's not do this, okay? Eduardo? Please? Eduardo? We can fix the problem another way." Except that at the same moment she was saying to me, somehow outside of this memory I have of these events, she was saying, "Do you understand what you're seeing?"

I said, "He's going to—"

"—Kill the guy."

"And that guy is?"

"Addict Number One."

"Who?"

"That guy is the first user," she said. "The very first one."

"And why is he important?"

Cassandra said, "For the sake of control. You don't get it, do you?"

"Tell me," I said.

"Addict Number One is being killed *in a memory.*"

Something coursed in me like a flash flood. A real perception, maybe, or just the blunt feelings of sympathetic drug abuse. When I tried to figure out the enormity of what Cassandra was telling me, I couldn't. I couldn't understand the implications, couldn't understand why she would tell me what she was telling me, because to talk was to die, as far as I could tell, because Fox was dead, Bob was dead, the Mnemonic X boys had been completely wiped out, probably fifty guys, all disappeared, same day, same time, reporters from my old paper were dead. Chasing the story of Albertine was to chase time itself, and time guarded its secrets.

"How's that possible? That's not possible! How are you going to kill someone in a memory? It doesn't make any sense."

"Right. It doesn't make any sense, but it happened. And it could happen again."

"But a memory isn't a *place.* It's nowhere but in someone's head. There's not a movie running somewhere. You can't jump up into the screen and start messing with the action."

"How do you know? Just watch and you'll see."

I was thinking, see, about the *diachronous theory.* The

pattern of abuse and dispersal of Albertine was widest and most threatening at the instant of the murder of Addict Number One, I was guessing, which was about to be revealed as a murder—the first and only murder, I hoped, that I ever needed to witness, because even if he was a smirking guy, someone unliked or ridiculed, even if he was just a drug addict, whatever, Addict Number One was *a prodigious rememberer.* As the first full-scale Albertine addict, I learned later, he had catalogued loads of memories, for example, *light in the West Village, which in July is perfect at sunset on odd-numbered streets in the teens and twenties.* It was true. Addict Number One had learned this. If you stood on certain corners and looked west in summer, at dusk, you would see that the city of New York had sunsets that would have animated the great landscape painters. Or how about the perfect bagel? Addict Number One had sampled many of the fresh bagels of the city of New York, and he compiled notes about the best bagels, which were found at a place on University and Thirteenth Street. They were large, soft, and warm. Addict Number One devoted pages to the taste of the bagel as it went into your mouth.

Sadly, instead of illuminating the life of Addict Number One, it's my job now to describe the pattern of the dispersal of his brains. The pattern that was exactly like the pattern of dispersal of radioactive material in lower Manhattan. Cortez held the revolver to the head of Addict Number One, whose expression of complete misunderstanding and disbelief was heartrending, enough so to prove that he had *no idea* what his murder meant, and Cortez pulled the trigger of the revolver, and Addict Number One fell over like he had never once been a living thing. *Fucking punk-ass junkie,* Cortez intoned. Were the baroque memories of Addict Number One now part of all that tissue splattered on the dog run in Tompkins Square? Was that a memory splashed on that retriever there, gunking up its fur, an electrical impulse, a bit of energy, withering in a pool of gore in a city park? I saw it because Cortez saw it, and Cortez gave the memory to Cassandra, who gave it to me: corpus callosum and basal ganglia on the dogs, on the lawn, and screaming women, the homeless army drawn up near, gazing, silent, as Addict Number One, slain by a drug dealer in memory only, weltered, gasping. His memories slain with him.

It was like this. Even though the memory was just a memory, its effect was *real*. As real as if it were all happening now. This is like saying that nine-tenths of the universe is invisible, I know. But just bear with me. Cortez's accomplishment was that, according to Cassandra, he'd learned from informers that Addict Number One was once a *real person*, with a *real past* (went to NYU, and his name was Paley, and he wanted to make movies), after which he'd located a picture of Addict Number One by reading an obituary from the time after Addict Number One was already dead.

Must have been pretty tempting to try to *fabricate* a memory about Addict Number One. *Oh yeah, I saw him on the Christopher Street pier that time.* Or *I saw him on my way to Hunts Point to visit my grandma.* Cortez may have tried this, perhaps a dozen times, skin-popping Albertine in an unfurnished room in East Harlem, vainly attempting to put a bullet in the head of an *imagined* encounter with Addict Number One, but no. Cortez had to go through every face in every crowd, all the remembered crowds of which he had ever been a part, every face passed on Broadway, every prone body on the Bowery, every body in the stands of Yankee Stadium. He shot more, spent most of the money from his bike messenger job on this *jones for narrative*, and then one day he was certain.

He was killing roaches in his empty apartment when suddenly he knew. He was prying up a floorboard to look for roaches and he knew. As certainly as he knew the grid of his city. He'd walked by Addict Number One one day, when he was sixteen, in Tompkins Square. Far from his own neighborhood. On his way to a game of handball. He'd walked by *him*, he knew it. Not someone else, but him, Addict Number One. *Guy looked like a faggot*, the way Cortez told Cassandra later. All white guys looked like faggots as far as he was concerned, and he'd just as soon kill the *punkass motherfucker* for looking like a faggot as for any other reason, although there were plenty of other reasons. Main thing was that if he could figure out a way to kill Addict Number One *in his memory*, then a whole sequence of events would *fail*, like when Addict Number One hooked up with certain black guys in his neighborhood who had been fronting heroin up until that time and gave to them the correct chemical compound of Albertine, the secrets of the raw materials needed for the manufacture, the apparatus. If Cortez killed his ass, this future would not turn out to be the *real* future. If Cortez killed his ass, then Cortez would control the syndicate.

It would take even more time and money, more time doping, a solid six months, in fact, in his room, going through that whole sequence of his life, like that time with his neighbor, he told Cassandra. Over and over again, Eduardo had to deal with that *drunken fuck neighbor*, not even gonna say his

name, Cortez would say to Cassandra, fighting off that memory when the guy, Eduardo's alleged uncle, in the rubble of an
abandoned building, exposed himself to little Eduardo, his
droopy uncut penis, fucking guy couldn't get hard no more,
looked like a gizzard, and the uncle drunkenly pronounced that
he was *lonelier than any man had ever been,* didn't belong in this
country, couldn't go back to the island nation of his birth,
no reason for a man to be as lonely as this man, no reason for
this surfeit of loneliness, every day in every way, and would
Eduardo make him feel *comfortable* for just this one day, treat
him like a loving man this one time, because he was so lonely,
had an aching in his heart that nothing could still, wouldn't
ask again, he swore, and took Eduardo, just a little *compadre,*
just a wisp, couldn't even lift an aluminum baseball bat,
couldn't lift a finger against the alleged uncle, took Eduardo
for his goddess—*you are my priestess, you are my goddess*—and
now Eduardo vowed that he would never suffer before any
man the way he had with the uncle.

The syringe, the eyedropper, the concentric rings of the
past. Again and again the uncle would attempt to seduce
him. He was willing to go through that, a thousand times if
he had to, until he had the gun on his person, in the waist-
band of his warm-up suit, and he was ready. He was sixteen,
with fresh tattoos, and he'd been to mass that morning and
he had a gun, and he was going to play handball, and he saw
this white faggot in the dog run, *and he just walked up to him
like they never met.* Though in truth it was like Eduardo Cortez knew him inside and out, and Eduardo wanted to make
something out of himself, his life that was so lost up until
then, where he was just a bike messenger, and the despera-
does of his neighborhood were all going to be working for

him, and if they made one wrong move, he'd throw them off a fucking bridge, *whatever bridges is still up*, and if they touched the little girls in his neighborhood, that was another crime, for which he would exact a very high price, a mortal price, and the first priority, the long-term business plan was that Eduardo Cortez would be the guy that would make profits from memories, even if his own memories were bad. That was just how it was going to go, and I saw all this with Cassandra, that Cortez had managed by sheer brute force to murder a memory, splatter a memory like it was nothing at all.

One minute Addict Number One was wandering in the East Village, years before he was an addict, years before there even was an Albertine to cop, and he was thinking about how he was going to get funding for his digital-video project, and then, right in front of a bunch of dog walkers, the guy *disappeared*. This is the story, from the point of view of those who were not in on the cascading of memories. It's one of the really great examples of public delusion when you read it in the online police records, like I did.

> *Witnesses insist that the victim, first referred to as*
> *Caucasian John Doe, later identified as Irving Paley of*
> *433 East 9th St, was present on the scene, along with a*
> *Hispanic man in his teens, and then, abruptly, no longer*
> *present. "It's as if he just vanished," remarked one witness.*
> *Others concur. No body located thereafter. Apartment also*
> *completely emptied, possibly by assailant.*

Good thing those records were stored on a server in Queens. Since One Police Plaza is dust.

The guys in the smelting plant were all wearing uniforms. They were the uniforms of bike messengers, as if the entire story somehow turned on bike messengers. Bike messenger as conveyor of meaning. There were these courtiers in the empire of Eduardo Cortez, and the lowest echelon was the beat cop, a phalanx of whom encircled the building, sending news of anyone in the neighborhood into command central by radio. And then there were the centurions of the empire, the guys in the bike messenger uniforms, wearing the crash helmets of bike messengers. All done up in Lycra, like this was some kind of superhero garb. When the elevator door swung back, it was clear that we had definitely penetrated to the inner sanctum of Eduardo Cortez, as if by merely thinking. And this inner sanctum was inexplicable, comic, and deadly. Sure, it was possible that I had now been researching for two weeks and no longer needed food or sleep in order to do it. Sure, maybe I was just doing a really great job, and, since I was an honest guy who seemed cool and nonthreatening, maybe I was allowed into places that the stereotypical Albertine abuser would not ordinarily be allowed. But it seemed unlikely. This was evidently one of the *fabled five mansions* of Cortez, among which he shuttled, depending on his whim, like a despot from the coca-producing latitudes.

"Eddie," Cassandra sang out into the low lighting of the smelting-plant floor, "I brought him like you said."

Which one was Eddie? The room was outfitted with gigantic machines, suspension devices, ramrods, pistons thundering, wheels turning, like some fabulous Rube Goldberg future, and there was no center to it, no throne, no black leather sofa with a leopard print quilt thrown over it, and none of the bike messengers in the room looked like the Cortez of my memory, the Cortez of Tompkins Square Park, on his way to play handball. Perhaps he'd had himself altered by a cosmetic surgeon with a drug problem and a large debt. In fact, in scanning the faces of the dozens of bike messengers in the room, it seemed that they all looked similar, all of European extraction, all harried, with brown hair on the verge of going gray, all with blue eyes, a little bit paunchy. Were they robots? Were they street toughs from the bad neighborhoods? They were, it turned out, the surgically altered army of Eddie Cortez foot soldiers, who made it possible for him to be in so many places at so many times, in all the *fabled five mansions*. Eddie was a condition of the economy now, not a particular person.

At the remark from Cassandra, several of the bike messengers gathered in the center of the room. Maybe they were all modified comfort robots, so that Eddie could use them professionally during the day and fuck them later at night. One of them finally asked, with a blank expression, "His writing any good?"

Cassandra turned to me. "They want to know if you're a good writer."

"Uh, sure," I said, answering to the room. "Sure. I guess. Uh, are you wanting me to write something? What do you have in mind exactly?"

More huddling. No amount of time was too lengthy, in terms of negotiation, and this was probably because time was no longer all that important to Cortez and the empire. All time present was now sucked up into the riptide of the past. Furthermore, since it was now possible that Eddie could disappear at any moment, like Addict Number One had, when someone else figured out his technique for dealing with the past, he had apparently deliberately moved to ensure an eternal boring instant where everybody looked the same and where nothing particularly happened. Events, any kind of events, were dangerous. Eddie's *fabled five mansions* featured a languid, fixed *now*. He took his time. He changed his appearance frequently, as well as the appearance of all those around him. That way he could control memories. So his days were apparently taken up with dye jobs, false beards, colored contact lenses, with shopping for items relating to disguise and imposture and disfigurement.

A bike messenger goon addressed me directly on the subject of writing about Albertine.

"Funny you should, uh, suggest it," I said. "Because I have been assigned to write a history, and that's why I got in contact with Cassandra in the first place. . . ."

Everyone looked at her. Faint traces of confusion.

Have I described her well enough? In the half light, she was a *goddess*, even though I figure addicts always shine in low lighting. In the emergency lighting of Eddie's lair, Cassandra was the doomed forecaster, as her name implied. She was the whisperer of syllables in a tricky meter. She was the possibility of possibilities. I knew that *desire* for me must have been a thing that was slumbering for a really long time. It was just desire for desire, but now it was ungainly. I felt some stirring of possible futures with Cassandra, didn't want to let her out of my sight. I was guilty of treating women like ideas in my search for Albertine. In fact, I knew so little about her that it was only just then that I thought about the fact that she was Asian too. From China, or maybe her parents or grandparents were from Hong Kong or Taiwan. Because now she swept back her black and maroon hair, and

I could see her face. Her expression, which was kind of sad.

They all laughed. The bike messengers. I was the object of hilarity.

"Cassandra," they said. "That's a good one. What's that, like some Chinese name?"

"You did good, girl. You're a first-class bitch, Albertine, and so it's time for a *treat*, if you want."

A broadcaster's voice. Like Eddie had managed to hire network talent to make his announcements.

"Wait," I said. "Her name is . . ."

And then I got it. They named it after her.

"You named the drug after her?"

"Not necessarily," the broadcasting voice said. "Might have named *her* after the drug. We can't really remember the sequence. And the thing is, there are memories either way."

"She doesn't look like an Albertine to me."

"The *fuck* you know, *canary*," the broadcaster said, and suddenly I heard Eddie in there, heard his attitude. Canary. A reporter's nickname.

Cassandra was encircled by bike messengers and hefted up to a platform in the midst of the Rube Goldberg devices. Her rags were removed from her body by certain automated machines, prosthetic digits, and she was laid out like a sacrificial victim, which I guess is what she was, one knee bent, like in classical sculpture, one arm was stretched above her head. No woman is more poignant than the woman about to be sacrificed, but even this remark makes me more like Eddie, less like a lover.

"Your pleasure?" a bike messenger called out.

"Slave Owner, please," said Cassandra.

"Good choice. Four horsepower, fifteen volts, three hundred fifty rpm."

I covered my ears with my hands, and except for the glimpse of the steel bar that was meant to raise her ankles over her head, I saw no more—for the simple reason that I didn't want to have to remember.

The bike messengers of the Cortez cartel had a different idea for me. I was led down a corridor to the shooting gallery. I was finally going to get my taste.

The guy holding my arms said, "Thing is, all employees got to submit to a mnemonic background check. . . ."

A week or so before, I'd read a pamphlet by a specialist in medicinal applications of Albertine. There's always a guy like this, right, a Dr. Feelgood, an apologist. He was on the Upper West Side, and his suggestion was that when getting high, one should always look carefully around the room and eliminate bad energies. *Set and setting*, in fact, were just as important with Albertine as with drugs in the hallucinogenic family:

> *If there's any scientific validity at all to the theories of C. G. Jung and his followers, there's genuine cause for worry when taking the drug known as Albertine. The reason for this is quite simply Jung's concept known as* collective unconsciousness.
>
> *What do we mean when we invoke this theory? We mean that under certain extraordinary circumstances it is possible that memory, properly thought of as the exclusive domain of an Albertine effect, can occasionally collide with other areas of brain function. As Jung supposed, we each harbor a register of the simulacra that is part of being*

*human. This fantasy register, it is said, can be the reposi-
tory for symbolisms that are true across cultural and
national lines. What kinds of images are these? Some of
them are good, useful images, such as any representation of
the divine: Christ as the Lamb of God, Buddha under the
Bodhi tree, Shiva, with his many arms. Each of these is
a useful area for meditation. However, images of the
demonic are also collective, as with depictions of witches.
The terrors of hell, in fact, have had a long collective
history. Now it appears that certain modern phantasms—
the CIA operative, the transnational terrorist—are both
"real" and collective.*

*Therefore, we can suggest that casual users of Albertine
make sure to observe some rules for their excursions. It's
important to know a little about whom you have with you
at the time of ingestion. It's important to know a little bit
about their own circumstances. To put it another way,
people you trust are a crucial part of any prolonged
Albertine experience.*

*I suggest five easy steps to a rewarding experience with
your memories: (1) Find a comfortable place; (2) Bring
along a friend or loved one; (3) Use the drug after good
meals or rewarding sexual experiences, so that you won't
waste all your time on the re-creation of these things;
(4) Keep a photo album at hand, in case you want to draw
your attention back to less harmful recollections; (5) Avoid
horror films, heavy metal music, or anything with occult
imagery.*

The advice of the good doctor was ringing in my ears.
No matter what happened to my city, no matter how many

incarnations of boom and bust it went through—the go-go times, the Municipal Assistance Corporation—shooting galleries persisted in the Hot Zone and elsewhere. The exposed beams, the crumbling walls, the complete lack of electricity and heat, windows shattered, bodies lying around on mattresses. If it was important to know and trust the people with whom I was going to use, I was in some deep shit. Who wouldn't dread coming here to this place of unwashed men, of human waste and dead bodies?

In the shadows, there was a guy with a stool and a metal folding table. I was motioned forward as the addict in front of me, an old hippie, collapsed onto the floor. Probably remembering the best night of sleep he ever had.

Behind me, operatives in the Cortez syndicate made sure that my step was sturdy.

"Give me your hand," the Albertine provider said in a kind of doomed murmur.

I looked at my hand. On that cheap table, no doubt the site of a hundred violent games of poker.

"Don't mind we kinda stay close?" said one of the goons. He used the choke hold. Another guy held my hand. This would be the gentle description. If they were worried about my getting away, they shouldn't have worried, because I was a reporter. But that wasn't the motive, it dawned on me. They were hoping to come along for the ride, if possible, to see what they needed to know about their collaborator, if that's what I was going to be. The historian of the empire.

"You don't honestly think you're going to be able to see what I see, do you?" I said. "There's just no way that works according to physics."

The needle went in between the tendons on the top of

my right hand. Blood washed back into the syringe. A bead pearling at my knuckle.

"First time, yo?" someone said.

"For sure," I said.

"Goes better if you're thinking about what you *want* to know. Chiming. Thinking of bells, bells from a church, that's what you need to think about, things get chiming, the pictures get chiming. Because if you think of stuff you *don't* want to know, then *bang*—"

Like I said, what I wanted to know first when I finally got dosed on Albertine was how I would do on this assignment. I mean, if you could see the future, which seemed like horseshit, but if that was really possible, then I wanted to know how my story turned out. Which I guess makes me a real writer, because a writer is someone who doesn't care about his own well-being when the story is coming due, he just cares about the story, about getting it done. I wanted to get the story done; I wanted to get it into the magazine. I wanted to be more than another guy who survived the blast. So that was the *memory* I wanted to live through on Albertine. But that doesn't describe the beginning of the trip at all. One second I was listening to the guy tell me about *chiming*, next moment there was a world beside the world in which I lived, a world behind the world, and maybe even a sequence of them lined up one behind the other, where crucial narratives were happening. The splinter hanging off the two-by-four next to the table seemed to have a world-famous history, where dragonflies frolicked in the limbs of an ancient redwood. And maybe this was the prize promised first by Albertine, that all things would have meaning. Suddenly there was discrimination to events, not all this disjunctive shit, like millions of people getting incinerated for no good reason. Instead: discrimination, meaning, value. The solarizing thing again, and I could hear the voices of the people in the room, but as if I were paralyzed, I was experiencing language as *material*, not as words but as something sludgy like molasses. Language was molasses. Life had been EQ'd badly, and all was high-end distortion, and then there was a tiling effect, and the grinning, toothless face of the guy who'd just shot me up was divided into zones, as if he were a painting from the modernist chapter of art history, and zones were sort of rearranged so he was a literal blockhead, and then I heard this music, as if the whole history of sounds from my life had become a tunnel under the present, and I could hear voices, and I could hear songs. I could pluck one out of the air, like I could pluck out some jazz from the 1950s—here's a guy banging on the eighty-eights, stride style—and when I selected it from the tunnel of memories, I could hear the things beside it, a concert that I had to go to in junior high, in the school auditorium, where some guys in robes demonstrated some Buddhist overtone singing. They were sitting on an oriental carpet—you know the mysteries of the world always had to have an oriental carpet involved—and we were all supposed to be mystical and wearing robes and shit, and beside me there was the voice of my friend Dave Wakabayashi, who whispered, "Man, we could be listening to the game," because there was a day game that day, right? What team? And who was pitching? And then the sound of Mandarin, which was exactly like a song to me, because of all the kinds of intonation that were involved in it, all those words that had the same sound but different intonations.

And after that accretion of songs, a flood of the smells from my life, barely had time to say some of them aloud, while my stool was tipping backward, in the shooting gallery, my stool was tipping backward, and the back of my head was connecting with some hard surface, *citronella*, *cardamom*, smell of melting vinyl, smell of a pack of Polaroid film, five kinds of perfume, smell of my grandfather dying, *meat loaf prepared from a box*, freshly cut lawns, the West Indian Day parade in New York City, which is the smell of curried goat, ozone right before a storm, diesel exhaust, the smell of having fucked someone for the first time, the shock of it, more perfumes, a dog that just rolled in something, city streets in July, *fresh basil*, chocolate-chip cookies, ailanthus trees, and just when I was getting dizzy from all the smells, and right about the moment at which I heard the guys from Eddie's team, in their mellifluous slang, saying *Take his damn money*, which they definitely were going to do now, because I could tell that my arms were thrown wide to the world, give me the world, give me your laser light show and your perfect memories, doesn't matter what they are, rinse me in your planetarium of memories, for I am ready as I have never been, all of my short life. All was rehearsal for this moment as observer of what has come before; my longing is for perception, for the torrents of the senses, the tastes, the languor of skin on skin. I was made for this trip, it felt good, it felt preposterously good, and I noticed absently that my cock was hard; actually, I'm a little embarrassed to say it now, but I realized in that moment that mastery of the past, even when drug induced, was as sexy as the vanquishing of loneliness, which is really what men in the city *fuck against*. Think about it, the burden of isolation that's upon us all day and night, and think about how that diminishes in the carnival of sex. It's the same on the Teen (the latest street abbreviation of the name of the drug), it's the same with *chiming*, and I was actually a little worried that I might come like that, lying on the floor of their shooting gallery with this guy standing over me, reaching into my hip pocket where there used to be a wallet, but there was no wallet now, just a couple of twenties to get me out of trouble, if it came to that. He wanted them and he took them. I wanted to yell *Get the fuck off me*, but I could feel the blobs of drool at the corners of my mouth, and I knew I could say nothing, I could say only yes, yes, yes. And when it seemed like that was the lesson of Albertine, bitch goddess—when I thought, well, this must be what you get for your twenty-five bucks, you get to see the light show of lost time—*and then I got up off the floor* and walked into the lobby of the *tits and lit* magazine that had hired me, except that they hadn't hired me, I guess, not like I believed. The matter was still up in the air, and I was in the line with a lot of people claiming to be writers, people with their plagiarized clip files, though why anyone would want to pretend to be a writer is beyond me. I was hoping, since I was the genuine article, that I might actually *get the call*. Out came this girl with blue hair, past the receptionist robot at the desk out front, saying my name, *Kevin Lee*, like it somehow magically rhymed with *bored*, and I got up, walked past all those people. I realized, yes, that I was going to get the assignment, because I was the guy who had actually written something. I was the genuine article, and maybe fate had it in store for me that I'd get out of the armory where I shared a cardboard box with a computer programmer from Islamabad who, despite the unfortunate fact of his nationality in the current political climate, was a good guy.

The girl had blue hair! The girl had blue hair! And she looked sort of like Serena, that babe with whom I once skipped school to drink on Boston Common, and there I was again, like never before, with Serena, slurring the words a little bit when I told her she was the first person who ever took the time to have a real conversation with me. First white chick. Because, I told Serena, people looked at an Asian kid in school, *they assumed he was a math and science geek; oh, he's definitely smarter than everyone else*, that's what I told her, such a sweet memory. Well, it was sweet up until she told me that she already had a boyfriend, some college dude. Why hadn't she told me before, didn't I deserve to be told, didn't I have some feelings too? No, probably I was an inscrutable kid from the East. Right? She didn't tell me because I was Chinese.

And I was in a bad spot, in a drug dealer's shooting gallery, probably going to be in really big trouble because if I didn't write something for the cartel about the history of Albertine, which was what they seemed to want, I was probably a dead Chinese kid, but I didn't care, because I believed I was drunk on the Boston Common, and I was reciting poetry for a beauty who would actually go on to be an actress in commercials, *There's a certain Slant of light, / Winter Afternoons—/ That oppresses, like the Heft / Of Cathedral Tunes*. I could recite every poem I'd ever memorized. It was amazing. Serena's face frozen in a kind of convulsive laughter, *You are some crazy bastard, Kevin Lee*. It was all good, it was all blessed, the trip. But then she said that thing about her boyfriend again, some would-be film-maker.

And I was back in the office with Tara, girl with the blue hair. "Jesus, Lee, what happened? You don't look so good. Why didn't you call me? When I gave you the assignment, I assumed you were a professional, right? Because there are a lot of other people who would have jumped at the chance to write this piece." Glimpse of myself in the reflection of her office window. The city smoldering out the window, the whole empty city, myself superimposed over it. I looked like I hadn't eaten in two weeks. The part of my face that actually grew a beard had one of those stringy insubstantial beards. My eyes were sunken and red. I had the bruises under my eyes. Whatever viscous gunk was still irrigating my dry mouth had hardened at the corners into a crust. I had nothing to say. Nothing to do but hand over the notes. Twenty-nine thousand words. Tara paged through the beginning with an exasperated sigh. "What the fuck do you think we're going to do with this, Kevin? We're a fucking porn magazine? Remember?" As in dreams, I could feel the inability to do anything. I just watched the events glide by. From this quicksand of the future. I could see Tara with the blue pencil to match her blue hair receding in the reflection in the window.

And then there were a dozen more futures, each as unpleasant as what I'd already seen. Breaking into the room of Bertrand, the administrator of the armory, stealing his beaker full of Teen, which he kept in his luxury fridge—he was the only guy in the entire armory who got to have a refrigerator—and being discovered in the process of stealing his drugs by a woman who'd just recently gone out of her way to ask me where my family was, why I was living here alone. Seeing her face in the light from the fridge, the only light in the room. She was wearing army fatigues, the uniform of the future, everyone in army fatigues, everyone on high alert. And then I jumped a few rich people up in Park Slope, an affluent neighborhood that wasn't obliterated in the blast; I was wearing a warm-up suit, I was jumping some guy carrying groceries, and suddenly I was awake, with my face in my hands.

The guys at the folding table were laughing.

I wiped my leaking nose on my wrists. Stood up on unsteady knees.

"Good time?" said the administerer of poisons. "You need the boost; everybody needs it afterwards. Don't worry yourself. You need the boost. To smooth it out."

He handed me a pill.

One of the security experts said to another: "Just the usual shit, man. Names of cheap-ass girls kiss his ass when he was just a little Chinese boy eating his mommy's *moo goo gai pan*. Same shit."

That was it? That was what I was to them? A bunch of sentimental memories? The predictable twenty-five-dollar memories that coursed through here every day? What were they looking for? Later, I knew. They were looking for evidence that I had dropped off files with government agencies or that I had tipped off rival gangs. And they were looking to see if I'd had contact with Addict Number One. They were looking to see what I had put together, what I knew, where my researches had taken me, how much the dark story of Albertine was already living in me, and therefore how much of it was available to you.

"Okay, *chump*," a bike messenger said to me. "Free to go."

The door opened, and down a corridor I went, wearing handcuffs, back the way I'd come, like I could unlearn what I had learned—that I had the taste for the drug, and that the past, except for the part I saw while high, was woefully lost. I'd been addicted by the drug overlord of my city, and I was standing on his assembly-line floor again, though now Cassandra, or whoever she was, was missing, and the voice of the Cortez television announcer rang out, observing the following on the terms of my new employment: "We want you to learn the origin of Albertine, we want you to write down this origin and all the rest of the history of Albertine, from its earliest days to the present time, and we don't want you to use any fancy language or waste any time, we just want you to write it down. And because what you're going to do is valuable to us, we are prepared to make it worth your while. We're going to give you plenty of our product as a memory aid, and we will give you a generous per diem. You'll dress like a man, you'll consider yourself a representative of Eddie Cortez, you'll avoid disrespectful persons and institutions. Remember, it's important for you to *write* and not worry about anything else. You fashion the sentences, you make them sound like how regular people talk, we'll look after the rest."

"Sounds cool," I said. "Especially since I'm already doing that for someone else."

"No, you *aren't* doing it for somebody else, you are doing it for us. Nobody else exists. The skin magazine doesn't exist, your friends don't exist. Your family doesn't exist. We exist."

I could feel how weak my legs were. I could feel the

sweat trickling down the small of my back, soaking through my T-shirt. I was just hanging on. Because that's what my family did, they hung on. My grandfather, he left behind his country. My father, you *never* saw the guy sweat. My mother, she was on a plane that had to make an emergency landing once; she didn't even give it a second thought, as far as I could tell. Representatives of the Cortez cartel were tracking me on a monitor somewhere, or on some sequence of handheld computers, watching me, and they were broadcasting their messages to staff people who could be trusted.

Who knew how many other people in the Eddie Cortez operation were being treated the way I was being treated today? Bring this guy into the fold, conquer him, if not, *neutralize him*, leave him out in the rubble of some building somewhere. It was an operation staffed by guys who all had guns, stun guns, and cattle prods, real guns with bullets that could make an abstract expressionist painting out of a guy like me, and I was trying to get the fuck out of there before I was dead, and I could barely think of anything else. Now they were taking me down this long hall, and it wasn't the corridor I was in before, because the building had all these layers, and it was hard to know where you were, relative to where you had been before, or maybe this is just the way I felt because of what the voice on the loudspeaker said next.

Remember to be vigilant about forgetting.

Which reminds me to remind you of the *diachronous theory of Albertine abuse patterns*, which of course recognizes *the forgetting* as a social phenomenon coincident, big-time, with a certain pattern of Albertine penetration into the population. The manifestation of *forgetting* is easy to explain, see, because it has to do with bolstering the infrastructure of memory elsewhere. Like anyone who's a drinker knows, you borrow courage when you're drinking; you are emboldened for the night but depleted in the morning. Addiction is about credit. That amazing thing you said at the bar last night, that thing you would *never* say in person to anyone, it's a one-time occurrence because tomorrow, in the light of dawn, when you are separated from your wallet and your money, when your girlfriend hates you, you'll be *unable* to say that courageous thing again because you are wrung out and lying on a mattress without sheets. You borrowed that courage, and it's gone.

So the thing with Albertine was that at night, under its influence, you *remembered*. Tonight the past was glorious and indelible—Serena in the park with the rum and the bittersweet revelation of her boyfriend—tonight was the beauty of almost being in love, which was a great beauty, but tomorrow your memory was full of holes. Not a blackout, more like a brownout. You could remember that you once knew things, but they were indistinct now, and the understanding of them just flew out the window. It was like the early part of jet lag, or Thorazine. *Why did I come into this room? I was going to get something.* Suddenly you had no idea, you stood looking at the pile of clothes in front of the dresser, clothes that were fascinating colors, that old pair of jeans, very interesting. *Look at that color. It's so blue.* Maybe you needed to do something, but you didn't, and you realized that things were going on in your body, and they were inexplicable to you. You were really thirsty. Maybe you ought to have had some juice, but on the way to the bottle of water on the table, you forgot.

The history of Albertine became a history of forgetting. A geometrically increasing history of forgetfulness. The men in charge of its distribution, by reason of the fact that they started using it for organizational reasons, to increase market share, they were as forgetful as the hard-core users, who after a while couldn't remember their own addresses, except occasionally, and who were therefore on the street, asking strangers, *Do you know my name? Do you happen to know where I live?* The history of the drug, requested by Cortez, was therefore important. How else to plan for the future? If the research and development team at Cortez enterprises didn't forget how to read, then, as long as they had a hard copy of the history, everything was cool. I would write the story; they'd lock it away somewhere.

Before I had a chance to agree or disagree, I was going down in the industrial elevator, alone, and it was like being shat out the ass of the smelting plant. It was dawn, with the light coming up under the lip of that relentless cloud. Dawn, the only time these days there was any glimmer on the horizon, before the debris clouds massed again. But listen, I have to come clean on something. I missed Cassandra. That's what I was feeling. She'd sold me out to Eddie Cortez, made me his vassal, like she was his vassal. Trust and fealty, these words were just memories. So was Cassandra, just a memory. A lost person. Who'd reassured me for a few minutes. Who'd have sold out anyone for more drugs and a few minutes on an industrial sex machine. Was I right that there was *something there?* For an Albertine second, the slowest second on the clock, it seemed that she was the threshold to some partially forgotten narrative, some inchoate past, some incomplete sign, like light coming in

through window blinds. Boy, I was stupid, getting sentimental about the mistress of a drug kingpin.

Daylight seemed serious, practical. It was the first time I
could remember being out in the daylight since I started
compiling these notes. On the way back to the armory, I
waited on the line up the block for the one pay phone that
still worked. Usually there were fifty or sixty people out
front. All of them simmering with rage because the connection was sketchy, the phone often disconnected, and everyone listened to the other callers, to the conversations. Imagine
the sound of the virtual automaton's computerized warmth:
*We're sorry, the parties you are contacting are unable to accept the
call.* Who was sorry exactly? The robot? Guy holding the
receiver shouted, "I need to know the name of that prescription! I'm not a well man!" Then the disconnection. A woman
begged her husband to take her back. Disconnection. And a
kid who had lost his parents, trying to locate his grandparents. Disconnection. The phone booth offered that multitude of sad stories.

Soon it was my turn, and my father got on, man of few
words.

"We told you not to call here anymore," he said.

"What?"

"You heard me."

"I haven't called in . . ."

I tried to put it all together. How long? Measuring time
had become sort of impossible. There was nothing to do but
make a stab at it.

". . . three weeks."

"We can't give you anything more. Our own savings are
nearly exhausted. You need to start thinking about how

you're going to get out of the jam you're in without calling us every time it gets worse. It's *you* who is making it worse. Understand? Think about what *you're* doing!"

I could see the people behind me in the pay phone line leaning in toward the bad news, excited to get a few tidbits. Their own scrapes were not nearly as bad.

"What are you talking about?"

"I've told you before," he said. "Don't raise your voice with me."

His own voice defeated, brittle.

"Put Mom on the line!"

"Absolutely not."

"Let me talk to Mom!"

Then some more nonsense about how I had caused my mother unending sorrow, that it was her nature only to sacrifice, but I had squandered this generosity, had stamped up and down on it with my callousness, my American callousness, as if my family had not overcome innumerable obstacles to get me where I was. I made the selflessness of my heritage seem like a deluded joke. I had dishonored him by my shameful activities, et cetera, et cetera. It was as bad as if I had *died during the blast.*

A bona fide patriarchal dressing-down, of a sort I thought I had left behind long ago. I was watching the faces of the people in the line behind me, and their faces were reflecting my own. Incredulity. Confusion.

"Dad, I have no idea what you're talking about. Listen to me."

"You can't call here every day with your preposterous lies. Your imagined webs of conspiracy. We won't have it. We are exhausted. Your mother cannot get out of bed, and

I am up at all hours frantic with worry about you. How are we supposed to live? Get some help!"

I smiled a befuddled smile for my audience, and I replaced the receiver. In midstream. Of course I hadn't called my parents recently, hadn't called them the day before, or the week before, or the week before that. Hadn't called them often at all. My crime, in fact, was that because of shame about where I lived and what I was doing, I didn't really call anyone anymore.

I looked at the next guy in line. A melancholy African American man, with a fringe of gray hair and eyeglasses patched with some duct tape. It was beginning to rain, of course, and I saw a blob of obsidian ooze splatter the surface of his glasses.

"I guess I just called them," I said. "I mean, I guess I forgot that I called them."

He pushed past me.

To forget was threatening now. Nobody wanted to have anything to do with a forgetter. A forgetter meant just the one thing. A forgetter had abscesses in his arms, or a forgetter had sold off the last of his possessions and was trying to sell them a second time because he had forgotten that the apartment was already empty. The highest respect, the most admiration, was accorded those with *perfect recall*—that was part of the *diachronous theory*, or if it wasn't yet, I predicted it would soon be part of that theory. Geeks with perfect recall would get up in public settings, with a circle of folding chairs around them, and then, in front of an amazed audience, these geeks would remember the perfect textures of things: *Ah yes, the running mates of the losers in the last eight presidential elections, let me see. And the names of their wives.*

And the weather on Election Day. Massive fraud would be per-petrated in certain cases, where these perfect-recall geeks would, it turned out, have needle tracks, just like the rest of us. *Ohmygod! They were doping*, and they would be escorted out into the street, in shame, where again rain was begin-ning to fall.

Which is why when I got back to the armory and found the package on my bed, I felt that pornographic thrill. I could manage an eyedropper as good as the next guy, right? I'd work up to the needles. What else was there to hang around for? No one was waiting for me. Maybe I could get back to the night before, when I was talking to Cassandra. I said this little preliminary prayer, *May this roll of the dice be the one in which I remember love*, or teen sex, or that time when I had a lot of money from a summer job and I was barbecuing out in the back of our unit, and everybody was drinking beer and hav-ing a good time.

I would become a junkie in a supply closet, and I would use a lantern I'd looted from a camping-equipment store af-ter the blast. I held the eyedropper above me, and the drop-let of intoxicant was lingering there, and I was the oyster that was going to envelop it and make it my secret. The drop in the dropper was like the black rain of NYC, which was like the money shot in a porn film, which was like the tears from the Balkan statuary of the Virgin in the naïf style. The lantern shone up from underneath my supply closet shelves, and there was that rush of perfumes that I've already de-scribed, which meant that it was all beginning again. I was lucky for the perfumes I've known; other guys just know paperwork, but I've known the smell of people right before being naked with them, what an honor. All junkies are lapsed idealists, falling away from things as they were. *I was a murderer of time*. I'd taken the hours of my life out back of the armory and shoved them in the wood chipper or buried them in a swamp or bricked them up in the basement. But this thought was overwhelmed by the *personal scent* of a fashion student who lived near us when I was in California. It was on me like a new atmosphere. Along with the sheets of fog rolling in over the bay.

It was all a fine movie. At least until something really horrible occurred to me, a *bummer* of a thought. How could it be? Thinking about Serena, again, see, on the Boston Common, drinking rum, remembering that she actually had Cherry Coke, not the soft drink once known as the Real Thing, to which I said, "Cherry Coke, girl, that's not Coke, because no Coke product that occurs, historically, after the advent of the New Coke—held by some to have been a reaction to sugar prices in Latin American countries—no Coke that occurs after that time is a legitimate Coke. Get it? The only Coke product that is genuine with respect to the rum and Cokes you're proposing to drink here is Mexican Coke, which you can still get in bottles and which still features some actual cane sugar." An impressive speech, a flirtatious speech, but somewhere in the middle of remembering it— and who knew how many hours had passed now, who knew how many days—this thought I mentioned occurred to me:

Serena's boyfriend, the guy she was seeing besides me, or instead of me, *was Addict Number One*.

Years before, I mean. Way before he was the actual Addict Number One. Because we were in high school then, and Addict Number One hadn't been killed yet, or hadn't vanished. Not in this version of the story. He was a college guy, and he wanted to make movies, went to NYU, lived downtown, wore a lot of black, just like Addict Number One. And he could tell you a lot about certain recordings that hardcore bands from Minneapolis made in the eighties, and he had a lot of opinions about architecture and politics and sitcoms and maybe bagels, I don't know. I could feel that it was true. It was a hunch, but it was a really good hunch. There was an intersection in the story, a convergence, where there hadn't been one before, and the intersection involved *me*, or at least tangentially it involved me. Before, I was an observer, but now I was coming to see that there was no observing Albertine. Because Albertine was looking back into you. The thought was so unsettling that I was actually shaking with terror about it, but I was too high to stop remembering.

Serena said, "You won't have any idea whether this is Coke or Cherry Coke after the first half a cup. I could put *varnish* in here, you wouldn't know." She smiled, and now I felt myself drunk just with the particulars of her smile. It was a humble, lopsided smile, and she was wearing those patched blue jeans, and she pulled off her green Dartmouth sweatshirt, to reveal a T-shirt with the sleeves cut off, the T-shirt advertising a particular *girl deejay*, and I could see the lower part of her belly underneath the T-shirt. And there was the slope of her breasts. Her smile promised things that never came to be, you know? While I was taking it in, turning over the irrefutable fact of her smile and the tiny series of beautiful lines, like parentheses, at the corners of her fantastic mouth, Serena began to fade. "Don't go," I said. "There's some stuff we need to cover," but it was like those cries in a dream, the cries that just wake you up. They don't actually bring help. They just wake you. I could see her fading, and in her stead, I saw a bunch of bare trees from some November trip to the malls of Jersey. *Autumn.*

I seized the eyedropper, which, because it had been sitting on my roach-infested mattress while I was busy remembering, now seemed to have black specks all over the tip of it, and maybe there was some kind of bug crawling around on there, I don't know. I held back my eyelids. I was aching in my eye sockets.

The plan was to summon her back, to *call her name* in the old psychoanalytic way, you know. Names count for something. Strong feelings count for something. And such a beautiful name anyhow, right? Serena, like some ocean of calm lapping against the fucked-up landscape. I would ask her. That is, I would ask if I were able to map the weird voyages of my younger self, that Asian kid trying to declare himself to a Yankee girl through really abstract, complicated poetry.

Because if it was really true that Cassandra had somehow willed me to see what she knew about Eddie Cortez, just because she wanted me to see it, even if telling me the truth about Eddie was somehow a danger to her position as his mistress, then it was true that love and the other passions were important orienting forces in the Albertine epidemic. Like Eddie, who chased Addict Number One through the dingy recesses of his brain simply in the breadth of his malice and greed. Maybe the rememberer, in the intoxication of remembering, was always ultimately tempted to reach out the hand, and maybe this rememberer could do so, if his passion was strong enough. How else to look at it? What else did I have to go on? Because a hundred thousand Albertine addicts couldn't be wrong. Because they were all chasing the promise of some lost, glittering, perfect moment of love. Because some of them must have reached that elysian destination in their flash floods of memory and forgetfulness. Because I sure loved Serena, because she had a lopsided smile, because she had nails called *lycanthrope*, because love is good when you have nothing, and I had nothing, except bike messengers watching my every move.

I didn't remember Serena, though. All I could remember was a bunch of really horrible songs from my childhood. In particular, "Shake Your Bon-Bon," a song that definitely had not aged very well. Sounds tinny, like the sampling rate is bad somehow—you know, those early sampling rates on digital music, really tinny. And here's that little synthesizer loop that's supposed to sound like the Beatles during their sitar phase, girl backup singers, the attempt to make the glamorous leading man sound as though he didn't prefer boys—fine, really, but why pretend, suck and fuck, man, knock yourself out. Seven hours, at least, passed in which I went over the minutiae of "Shake Your Bon-Bon." The utterly computerized sound of it, the vestiges of humanness in its barren musical palette, as if the singer dude couldn't be bothered to repeat the opening hook himself, no way, it'd sound better if they just looped it on Pro Tools, and then the old-fashioned organ, which was a simulated organ, et cetera, and the relationship between the congas and the guitars, okay, and what about that Latin middle section! Demographically perfect! So twentieth century! I didn't want to think about the trombone solo at the end of "Shake Your Bon-Bon," buried in the back, that sultry trombone solo, but I *did* think about it, about the singer's Caribbean origins oozing out at the edges of the composition, and his homosexuality. Went on this way for a while, including a complete recollection of a remix that I think I heard only one time in my entire life, which was in some ways the superior version, because the more artificial the better, like when they take out all the rests between the vocal lines, so that the song has effectively become *impossible to sing*. Nowhere to take a breath. Was anyone on earth thinking about the singer in question, these days after the blast? I bet no one at all was thinking of him, except for certain stalkers from Yonkers or Port Chester. Where was he exactly? Had he managed to find refuge in a hotel in South Beach before the blast? And were his memories of showbiz dominance so great that the big new out-of-state market for Albertine was seducing him now like everyone else? Was South Beach falling into the vortex of memory like New York before it?

Just when it seemed that I would never cast my eyes on Serena again, just when it seemed that it was all Ricky Martin from now on, she was *a vision before me*, you know, a thing of ether, a residuum, like lavender, like coffee regular. The odd thing was I got so used to remembering that one portion of our time together that I forgot what came later. I forgot that just because she had this boyfriend, this college dude with *short eyes*, this college man who chased after teens, didn't mean that I stopped talking to her altogether, because the attachments you have then, when you're a kid, at least back before the trouble in the world began, these friendships are the one sustaining thing. I could see myself in some institutional corridor, high school passageway, and there she was, golden in the light of grimy shatterproof windows, as if women and light were as close as lungs and air. I was slumped by a locker. Serena came across the corridor, across speckled linoleum tiles, and it seemed I had never looked at those tiles before, because she was wearing a certain sweatshop-manufactured brand of sneakers, and so I saw the linoleum, because the linoleum was improved by her and her sneakers.

"You okay?"

No. I was hyperventilating. Like I did back then. Anything could set me off. College entrance examinations, these caused me to hyperventilate, any dip in my grades. And I didn't tell anyone about it. Only my mother knew. I was an Asian kid and I was supposed to be incredibly smart. I was supposed to have calculus right at my fingertips, and I was supposed to know C++ and Visual Basic and Java and every other fucking computer language, and all this made me hyperventilate.

I said, "Tell me the name of the guy you're seeing. I just want to know his name. It's only fair."

"You really want to talk about this again?"

"Tell me once."

Battalions of teens slithered past, wearing their headphones and their MP3 players, all playing the same moronic dirge of niche-marketed neogrunge shit.

"Paley," she said. "First name Irving, which I guess is a really weird name. He doesn't seem like an Irving to me. Is that enough?"

God sure put the big curse on Chinese kids, because when the raven of fate flew across their hearts, they just couldn't show it. We were supposed to be shut up in our hearts because to be otherwise was not part of the collective plan, or maybe that was just how I felt about it. I felt like my heart was an overfilled water balloon, and I was hyperventilating.

"Kevin," she said, "you have to do something about the panic thing. They have drugs for it. You know?"

Do you know how much I think about you? I wanted to say. Do you want to know how you are preserved for all of human history? Because I have written you down, I have got down the way you pull your sweater sleeves over your hands, I have got down the way your eyeliner smudges. I have preserved the rollout on the heels of your expensive sneakers, which you don't replace often enough. I know about you and nectarines, I know you like them better than anything else, and I know that you aren't happy first thing in the morning, not without *a lot* of coffee, and that you think your shoulders are fat, but that's ridiculous. All this is written down. And the times you yelled at your younger sister on the bus, I wrote down the entire exchange, and I don't want anything for it at all. I don't want you to feel that there's any obligation attached, except that you made me want to use writing for preservation, which is so great, because then I started preserving other things, like all the conversations I heard out in front of the Museum of Fine Arts, and I started describing the Charles River, racing shells on the Charles, I have written all of this down too, I have written it all down because of you.

This was enough! This was enough to redeem my sorry ass, because suddenly all the moments were one, this moment and that, lined up like the ducks in some Coney Island shooting game, *chiming* together, and I said, "Serena, I've only got a second here, so listen up, I don't know any other way to put it, so just listen carefully. Something really horrible is going to happen to your friend Paley, so you have to tell him to stay out of Tompkins Square Park, no matter what, tell him never to go to Tompkins Square Park, tell him it's a reliable bet and that maybe he should do his graduate work at USC or something. I'm telling you this because I just know it, so do it for me. I know, I know, it's crazy, but do like I say."

At which point I was shaken rudely awake. *Oh, come on.* It was a time-travel moment. It was a memory-inside-a-memory moment, except that it might have been actually *happening.* I just wasn't sure. One of the bike messengers from Cortez Enterprises smacked me in the face. In my supply closet. I'd have been happy to talk, you know, but I was too high, and as so many accounts in the Albertine literature have suggested, trying to talk when you are high is like having all the radio stations on your radio playing at the same time. I could just make out the nasty sound of his voice in the midst of a recollected lecture from my dad on the best way to bet on blackjack. *Lee, you are not attending to your duties.* Not true, I tried to say, I'm a devoted employee, just got back here an hour ago, and I'm doing some more researches, and I'm finding out some very interesting things, there is a lot of stuff going on, I'm learning more and more.

"You haven't produced shit," said the bike messenger. "We need to see some results. You need to be e-mailing us some attachments, Mr. Lee, and so far we haven't seen anything."

"Just so incorrect," I said.

And my father said, *Never take the insurance bet; it's just not a good bet.*

"I've been taking some notes. Somewhere around here. There are all kinds of notes."

There was the digital recorder, for example, but the batteries were dead.

"This conversation isn't going very well," replied the bike messenger. "We have also heard that you have been moving product given to you as part of our agreement."

"There's just no way!"

"Don't make us have to remind you about the specifics of your responsibilities."

"Give me a break," I said. "I'm smarter than that."

Now the bike messenger flung open the door that led out beyond my supply closet. As if I had forgotten there was a world out there. And standing out in the hall was Tara from the *tits and lit* magazine, except she looked really disheveled, like she didn't want to be seen by anyone else in the hallway, and I said, "Tara, what are you doing here? I thought I had at least another couple weeks—"

"Look, you said you had the dropper; I don't know anything about all this. I gave you the money, so can I please just have the drugs? Then I'll get the fuck out of here."

I made some desperate pleas to the Cortez employee, looking at him looking at Tara, and Tara stood and watched. I stalled, demanded to know if there was a way for me to be sure that these guys, the bike messenger and Tara, weren't just figments of some future event that I was now "remembering," according to that theory about Albertine.

"Did you or did you not assign me an article about Albertine?"

Tara said, "Just set me up and let me get out of here."

And then Bertrand, the guy who doled out the habitable spaces in the armory, he got into the act too. Standing in the doorway, covered in grime, like he'd just come from his job at a filling station, except that as far as I knew it was just that Bertrand was an addict and had given up on personal hygiene. He gazed at me with make-believe compassion.

"Kevin, listen, we've given you chances. We've looked the other way. We've been understanding for months. We've made excuses for you. We pulled you out of the gutter when you were passed out there. But people living here at the armory are afraid to walk by your apartment now. They're just afraid of what's going to happen. So where does that leave us?"

Even Bob, my early source of information, was standing behind Bertrand, his hands on his hips. Trying to push past the throng of accusers, to get to me.

This was a moment when thinking carefully was more important than hallucinating. But because of the extremely dangerous amount of Albertine that was already overwhelming both my liver and my cerebral activity, reality just wasn't a station that I could tune. What I mean is, I went down under again. Right in front of all those people.

Soon I was hanging out on some sunporch in a subdivision in Massachusetts. All the houses, in whichever direction I turned, looked exactly the same. I bet they had electric fireplaces in every room. It was like CAD had come through with a backhoe, bulldozed the whole region into uniformity. I could remember each tiny difference, each sign that some person, some family, had lived here for more than ten minutes. Serena's folks had a jack-o'-lantern on the porch. And over there was a guy with one arm mowing the common areas. That intoxicating smell of freshly cut grass. The sound of yellow jackets trying to get in through the screen.

Serena was reiterating that I had said something *really*

scary to her at school today, and she needed to know if I'd said what I had said because of the *panic thing*. Were my symptoms causing me to say these crazy things, and if so, wouldn't it be better if I told someone what was happening instead of carrying it around by myself? She knew, she said, about really dangerous mental illnesses, she knew about these things and she wanted me to know that I would still be her friend, her *special friend*, even if I had one of those mental illnesses; so I was not to worry about it. And now would I please try to explain.

"Listen, I know what I said, and there's no reason you should believe me," I tried, "but the fact is that the only reason I can explain to you about the future is because *I'm in the future*. And in the future I know how much you mean to me. In the future, this four months that we're close, it keeps coming back around, again and again, like that day we were on Boston Common. It keeps coming back around. I could tell you all this stuff about the future, about New York City and how it gets bombed into rubble, about drugs, the epidemic that's coming, I could tell you how strung out I'm going to get. But that's not the point. Somehow *you're the point*. Serena, you're the trompe l'oeil in the triptych of the future, and that's because you know that guy. Paley. So you have to believe me, even though I probably wouldn't believe me if I were you. Still, the thing is, you have to tell him what I've told you. Maybe none of this will happen, this stuff; I sure hope not. Maybe it will all turn out different, just because I'm telling you. But we can't plan on that. What we have to plan on is your telling Paley that he's in danger."

"Actually, Kevin, what I think we need to do is talk to your mom."

The jack-o'-lantern on the porch, of course. It was autumn, which was bad news, which meant I was on the come down and in need of a boost, and the whole scene was swirling away into an electromagnetic dwindling of stories. Serena was gone, and suddenly instead of being back in my room at the armory, where, suspended in a lost present, I was about to be evicted from my supply closet, I was back doing my job, the job of journalist, and what a relief. I had no idea what day it was. I had no idea if I was remembering the past or the future, or if I happened to be in the present. Albertine had messed with all that. I was confused. So was the guy I was interviewing, who happened to be the epidemiologist with the theory about the Albertine crisis, the one I told you about earlier, except that he was no epidemiologist at all. That was just his cover story. Actually, he was the anthropologist Ernst Wentworth, and we were in his office at Brooklyn College, which wasn't really an office anymore, because there were about thirty thousand homeless people living on campus. At night there were vigilante raids in which the Arabic people living on one quad would be driven off the campus, out onto the streets of the Hot Zone, where stray gunshots from Eddie Cortez's crew took out at least two or three a night. It was trench war. No one was getting educated at Brooklyn College, and Wentworth was crowded into a single room with a half dozen other desks and twice as many file cabinets pushed against the windows.

He was having trouble following the interview. Me too. I couldn't remember if I had already asked certain questions:

Q: Check. Check. Check. Uh, okay, do you know anything about the origin of Albertine?

A: No one knows the origin, actually. The most compelling theory, which is getting quite a bit of attention these days, is that Albertine *has* no origin. The physicists at the college have suggested the possibility that Albertine owes her proliferation to a recent intense shower of interstellar dark matter. The effect of this dark matter is such that time, right now, has become completely porous, completely randomized. Certain subatomic constituent particles are colliding with certain others. This would suggest that Albertine is a side effect of a space-time difficulty, a quantum indeterminacy, rather than a cause herself, and since she is not a cause, she has no origin, no specific beginning that we know of. She just *tends to appear*, on a statistical basis.

Q: Given that this is a possibility, why are Albertine's effects only visible in New York City?

A: The more provocative question would be, according to quantum indeterminacy, does New York City actually exist? At least, if you take the hypothesis of theoretical physics to its logical conclusion. This would be a brain-in-the-vat hypothesis. NYC as an illusion purveyed by a malevolent scientist. Except that the malevolent scientist here is Albertine herself. She leads us to believe in a certain New York City, a New York City with post-apocalyptic, post-traumatic dimensions and obsessions. And yet perhaps this collective hallucination is merely a way to rationalize what is taking place: that it is now almost impossible to exist in linear time at all.

Q: So maybe in Kansas City they have similar hallucinations. Kansas City is the center of some galloping drug epidemic. And the same thing in Tampa or Reno or Harrisburg?

A: Could be. Something like that. *(Pause.)* Can I borrow some of your—?

Q: There's only a little left. But, sure, get a buzz on. *(Getting serious.)* Have you attempted a catalogue of types of Albertine experiences?

A: Well, sociopaths seem to have a really bad time with the drug. We know that. And it's a startling fact, really. Since much of the distribution network is controlled by sociopaths. But at most dosage thresholds, sociopaths have stunted Albertine experiences. They'll remember their driver ed exam for hours on end. By *sociopaths*, I'm refer-ring especially to individuals with poor intrapsychic bonding, poor social skills. Individuals who lack for compassion. It would be hard to imagine them taking much pleasure in Albertine. On the other hand, at the top end of the spectrum are the ambiguous experiences of which you are no doubt aware. People who claim to remember future events, people who claim to remember other people's memories, people who claim to have interacted with their memories. And so forth. At first we believed that these experiences, which characterized many of the people here conducting our studies—myself included—were only occurring, if that's the right word, among the enlightened. That is, we believed that *ahistori-cal remembering* was an aspect of wish fulfillment among the healthiest and most engaged personalities. But then we learned that malice, hatred, and murderous rage could be just as effective at creating these episodes. In either case, we became convinced that the frequency of these reports merited our attention. If true, the fact of *ahistorical remembering* would have to suggest that the fabric of time is not woven together as consistently as we once thought. We tried at first to analyze whether these logically impossible experiences were "true" on a factual level, but now we are more interested in whether they are repeatable, visible to more than one person, et cetera.

Q: Does your catalogue of experiences shed any light on Albertine's origin?

A: One compelling theory that's making the rounds among guys in the sciences here at the college is that Albertine has infinite origins. That she appeared in the environment all at once, at different locations, synchronously, according to some kind of philosophical or metaphysical randomness generator. There's no other perfect way to describe the effect. According to this view, the disorder she causes is so intense that her origin is concealed in an effacement of the moment of her origin, because to have a single origin violates the parameters of nonlinearity. Didn't we already *do* this part about the origin?

Q: Shit. I guess you're right. Okay, hang on. *(Regroups.)* Do you, do you think it's possible to manipulate the origin of Albertine, to actually *control* the drug so as to alter a specific narrative? Like, say, the rise of the Albertine crime syndicate?

A: Sure, persons of my acquaintance have done plenty of that. At least on an experimental basis. We have had no choice. But I'm not at liberty to go into that today.

Q: Let's go back to the issue of what to do about the epidemic. Do you have a specific policy recommendation?

A: I did have some good ideas about that. *(Ponders.)* Okay, wait just a second. I'm going to look through my papers on the subject here. *(Riffles mounds on desk.)* I'm forgetting so much these days. Okay, my observation is that Albertine finds her *allure* in the fact that the human memory is, by its nature, imperfect. Every day, in every way, we are experiencing regret over the fact that we can conjure up some minimal part of the past, but not as much as we'd like. This imperfection of memory is built into the human animal, and as long as it's an issue, the Albertine syndicates will be able to exploit it. Strategies for containment have to come from another direction, therefore. Which is to say that the only thing that could conceivably help in the long run would be to make distribution of the drug extremely widespread. We should make sure everybody has it.

Q: How would that help?

A: Since Albertine has forgetfulness as a long-term side effect, it's possible that we could actually make everyone *forget that Albertine exists.* It would have to be concerted, you understand. But let me make an analogy. At a certain point in heroin addiction, you no longer feel the effects of the opiate, you only service the withdrawal. A similar effect could take place here. At a certain point, everyone would be trying to avoid the forgetting because they can't work effectively, they can't even remember where *work is*, and yet soon this forgetting would begin to invade even the drug experience, so that what you remember grows dimmer because you are beginning to accelerate plaque buildup and other anatomical effects. With enough of this forgetting, everyone would forget that they were addicts, forget that they needed the drug to remember, forget that memory was imperfect, and then we would be back to some kind of lowest common denominator of civic psychology. Damaged but equal.

Q: How would you go about doing this?

(Ernst Wentworth gives the interviewer the once-over in a way he has not done before.)

A: We're going to put it in the water supply.

Q: Hasn't that been tried already?

A: What do you mean?

Q: I think someone told me that an attack on the water supply was recently thwarted.

A: Are you serious?

Q: Well, unless someone was using disinformation—

Wentworth shouts:

A: Guys, you recording all of this?

The room was bugged, of course, and on this signal a bunch of academics rushed into Wentworth's office, blindfolded me, and carried me out. I didn't struggle. When I was freed, I was in the Brooklyn College astronomy lab. It was Ernst Wentworth who gently removed my blindfold.

"You understand we have no choice but to take every precaution. Just a couple of days ago, Claude Jannings, from the linguistics department, watched his wife disappear in front of him. She was there, in the kitchen, talking about the dearth of political writings pertaining to the Albertine epidemic, and then she was *gone*, just absolutely gone. As if someone were listening to the conversation the whole time. Apparently, her remarks about Albertine and inchoate plans to write on the subject were enough to make her a target."

My eyes became accustomed to the dim light of the astronomy lab. The interior was all concrete, functional, except for the platform where you could get up and take a gander at the heavens. Around me, there was a circle of guys in tweed jackets and cardigan sweaters. I saw a couple of bow ties. Khaki slacks.

"Wow, it's Kevin Lee! Right here in our lab!" Some good-natured chortling.

Huh?

Wentworth ventured some further explanations. "We've developed a technique for marking events so we don't forget later. Whenever one of us goes out in public, we bring along a poster or sign indicating the date and time. That way, if we travel backward on Albertine in search of particular events, we aren't thrown off or beguiled by unimportant days. And we bring clothing of various colors, red for an alert, green for an all clear. It's a conspiracy of order, you understand, and that's a particularly revolutionary conspiracy right now. What we've additionally found, by cataloguing memories—and we have guys who are medicated twenty-four hours a day thinking about all this—is that there are certain people who turn up over and over. We refer to people who are present at large numbers of essential Albertine nodal points as *memory catalysts*. Eduardo Cortez, for example, is a memory catalyst, and not in a good way. And there are some other very odd examples I could give you. A talk show host from ten or fifteen years ago seems to turn up quite a bit, perhaps just because his name is so memorable, *Regis Philbin*. You'd be surprised how close to the entire inner workings of the Albertine epidemic is Regis Philbin. When we're around

Philbin, we are always wearing red. We don't know what he means yet, but we're working on it. And then there's you."

"Me?"

One doctoral candidate, standing by the base of the telescope, nonchalant, spoke up. "If we had baseball cards of the players in the Albertine epidemic, you'd be collectible. You'd be the power-hitting shortstop."

"We have a theory," Wentworth said. "And the theory is that you're important because you're a writer."

"Yeah, but I'm not even a very good writer. I'm barely published."

Wentworth waved his plump hands.

"Doesn't matter. We've been trying to find out for a while who originally came up with your assignment. It wasn't your editor, Tara. That we know. She's just another addict. It was someone above her, and if we can find out who it is, we think we'll be close to finding a spot where the Frost Communications holding company connects to Cortez Enterprises. Somewhere up the chain, you were being groomed for this moment. Unless you are simply some kind of emblem for Albertine. That's possible too, of course."

Wentworth smiled, so that his tobacco pipe–stained teeth showed forth in the gloomy light. "Additionally, you're a hero from the thick, roiling juices of the New York City melting pot. And that is very satisfying to us. You want to see? We know so much about you that it's almost embarrassing. We even know what you like to eat and what kind of toothpaste you use. Don't worry, we won't put it on a billboard."

Later, of course, the constituency of the Brooklyn Resistance was a matter of much speculation. There were women there too, with mournful expressions, as though they had come along with the Resistance though they had grave doubts about its masculine power structure. Women in modest skirts or slightly unflattering pantsuits, like Jesse Simons, the deconstructionist, who argued that doping the water supply was embracing *the nomadic sign system of Albertine*, which of course represented not some empirical astrophysical event but rather a symbolic reaction to the crisis of instability caused by American imperialism. And there were a couple of African Americanists, wearing hints of kinte cloth with their tweeds and corduroys. They argued for intervention in the economic imperatives that led to drug dealing among the inner-city poor. And there was the great postcolonialist writer Jean-Pierre Al-Sadir. He argued that the route to victory over civic chaos was infiltration of the Albertine cartels. However, Al-Sadir, because of his Algerian passport, had been mentioned as part of the conspiracy that detonated the New York City blast. Still, here he was, fighting with the patriots, if that's what they were. It was a testament to the desperation of the moment that none of these academic stars would normally have agreed on anything, you know? I mean, these people hated one another. If you'd gone to a faculty meeting at Columbia three years ago, you would have seen Al-Sadir call Simons an *arrogant narcissist* in front of a college president. That kind of thing. But infighting was forgotten for now, as the Resistance began plotting its strategies. Even when I was hanging around with them, there would be the occasional argument about the semiotics of wearing red, or about whether time as a system was inherently phallogocentric, such that its present adumbrated shape was preferable as a representation of labial or vaginal narrative space.

"So you guys probably have one of those dials on a machine where we can go right to a direct year and day and hour and second, right?"

"Fat chance," Wentworth said. "In fact, we have a room next door with a lot of cots in it—"

"A shooting gallery?"

"Just so. And we employ a lot of teaching assistants, keep them comfortable and intoxicated for a long time and see what happens. Whatever you might think, what we have here is a lot of affection for one another, so a lot of stories go around like lightning, a lot of conjecture, a lot of despair, a lot of elation, a lot of plans. You know? We see ourselves as junkies for history. Of which yours is one integral piece. Let's go have a look, shall we?"

It would be great if I could report that the shooting gallery of the Resistance was significantly better than the Cortez shooting gallery, but really the only difference was that they sterilized the needles after each use and swabbed their track marks. No abscesses in this crowd. Otherwise, it was only marginally more inviting. Some of the most important academics of my time were lying on cots, drooling, fighting their way through the cultural noise of fifty years—television programming, B movies, pornography, newspaper advertisements—in order to get back to the origin of Albertine, *bitch goddess*, in order to untangle the mess she'd made. The other thing was that these guys were synthesizing their own batches of the stuff instead of buying it on the street, and when a bunch of chemists and biologists get into mixing up a drug, that drug *chimes*, let me tell you. They explained the chemical derivation to me too. Which looked kinda like this:

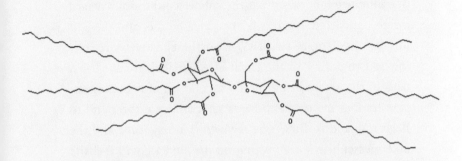

Apparently, the effect had to do with increasing oxygenated blood flow to neurotransmitters, thereby increasing electrical impulses. It wasn't that hard to do at all. Miraculous that no one had done it before now. The only physiognomic problem with Albertine was her tendency to burn out the cells, like in diseases of senescence. Albertine was sort of the neurochemical equivalent of steroid abuse.

I was lucky. Jesse Simons volunteered to be the prefect for my trip, and she and Wentworth stood awkwardly in the center of the room as a grad student from the Renaissance Studies department pulled the rubber tie around my arm. It was the sweetest thing, tying off again. I didn't care anymore about writing, I only cared about the part where I stunned myself with Albertine. I was dreaming of being ravished by her, overwhelmed by her instruction, where perception was a maelstrom of time past, present, and future. The eons were neon, they were like the old Times Square, of which it is said that the first time you ever saw it, you felt the rush of its hundreds of thousands of images, and I don't mean the Disney version, I mean the version with hookers and street violence and raving crack fiends. Albertine was like a soup of NYC neon. She was a catalogue of demonic euphonies. I felt the rubber cord unsnap, heard a sigh beside me, felt Jesse's arms around me, and the soft middle of sedentary Ernst Wentworth. Then we were rolling and tumbling in the thick of Albertine's forest. I was back in the armory, and there was a bunch of bike messengers leading me out, and I was screaming to Tara, and to Bertrand, and to Bob, *Save my notes, save my notes*, and the bike messengers were beating on me, and I could feel the panic thing in my chest, I could feel it, and I said, *Where are you taking me?* I passed a little circle of residents of the armory, carrying home their government rations of mac and cheese, not a hair on the head of any of them, all the carcinogenic residents of the armory, all of them with appointments for chemo later in the week, and *they were all wearing red.* I heard a voice, like in a voice-over: *We're sorry that you are going to have to see this. It was better when you had forgotten all about it.* And the bike messengers took me on a tour of Brooklyn in their Jeep, up and down the empty streets of my borough, kicking my ass the whole way, until my lips were split and bleeding, until my blackened eyes were swollen shut. We came to a halt down on the waterfront, on the piers. They dumped me out of the Jeep while it was still moving, and my last pair of jeans was shredded from all the broken glass and rubble. My knees and hips were gashed, but the syndicate wasn't through with me yet; some more of Cortez's flunkies took me inside a factory, a creepy institutional place, *where they manufactured the drug.*

Here it was. The Albertine sweatshop. There weren't

many buildings left in downtown Brooklyn, you know, because it was within the event horizon of the dirty bomb; a lot of the stuff on the waterfront was rubble. But this building was still here somehow, which implied that Eddie Cortez was subjecting his production staff to radioactive hazards. That was the least of it, of course, because most of the staff was probably high. Maybe that was the one job benefit.

"What are we doing here?" I asked the goons leading me past the surveillance gate and in through a front hall that looked remarkably like the reception area of the *tits and lit* magazine that had assigned my Albertine story in the first place. There was even one of those remote-control reception robots, just like at the magazine offices.

"Your questions will be answered in due course."

"Really? Because I have a big backlog."

"Don't get smart; we *will* make it hurt, dig?"

More corridors, linkages of impossible interiors, then into an office. We were waved through without hesitation. The women and men in the typing pool with expressions of abject terror on their faces. Guys in red sweaters in every room, red neckties, matching socks. We passed a troika of potted ferns, and I was congratulating Eddie, silently, for using his ill-gotten profits for quality-of-life office accessories like the potted palms, when I noticed an administrative assistant I recognized.

Deanna. Remember her? If you don't, you should lay off the sauce, gentle reader, because she was the character who told me about *the plot to poison the water supply*. The character who later became a hooker down by the Gowanus Canal. Have to say, considering the state of most of the people in the boroughs, Deanna was looking really great. I mean, she must have had some reconstructive dentistry, because back when I interviewed her, she had fewer teeth than fingers. Now she had on kind of a slinky silk blouse and what looked from this angle like a miniskirt. She still had long sleeves, of course. We recognized each other at the same moment, with a kind of disgust. I saw her eyes widen, I saw her look quickly around herself. To make sure no one had noticed. Was she working for Eddie now? Was she another employee drafted into the harem?

Then in the kind of frozen moment that can only happen in an era of completely subjective time, I began to understand that there was a commotion beginning around me, a commotion that had to do, I think, with Jesse Simons and Ernst Wentworth, who had remained so silent during the prior hour of kidnapping and torture that I had forgotten they were orbiting around me at all. They knew, I'd learned, what I knew; they saw what I saw. And I heard Jesse say to Ernst, *No, I have to do it; she's a woman; I don't want to hear about any guys shooting any women.* And Jesse Simons strode out of my memory, giving me a mournful glance on the way. Jesse, turns out, was carrying an enormous pistol with a silencer on the end, and as soon as she was on the scene, I could see the Cortez guys also moving into position with their submachine guns; there was a lot of yelling, someone was yelling *Get him out of here, get him out of here,* as if by removing me from the room, it would take Deanna out of the picture, out of the story. I hung on to a desk. They beat on me with the butt end of a submachine gun, and I looked up just in time to see Deanna, whatever her surname was, if she even had a surname, *disappear* at the muffled hiss and report of the silencer. The spot where Deanna had been sitting was emptied, and a plastic tape dispenser that she'd been holding in her hand was suspended briefly in midair. It fell to the wall-to-wall with a muffled thud. The men and women in the typing pool sent up a scream; many hands fluttered to mouths. And that was when Cortez's people opened fire on the room. Cleaning out as many witnesses as they could get. As with Jesse and Ernst, who didn't want to leave Deanna alive to inform on their plan, Cortez didn't want any mnemonic jockeys recalling the scene. As if the solution to the disorder of time was the elimination of all possible perceivers of time. I want to allow a dignified space in the story where the Cortez typing pool was massacred, so if I move on with the facts, don't think that I don't know that all those people had families. Because I know.

Someone got hold of my feet—when I tried to make a quick escape myself—and they were swearing at me, dragging me down the corridor toward some blank, faceless office, where I too would be killed. Meanwhile, Ernst Wentworth, like the angelic presence that he was, had the job of explanation: "Deanna knew about the trip to the water supply on which we're embarking now, with many thanks to you for helping us to close the loophole. You were the only person who knew the identity of this informer. Jesse is sticking with you for the last few minutes because there's one more thing you have to learn before you're done, and then, Kevin, you're a free man, with a load of forgetting in your future. I hope you write comic books or start a rock-and-roll band in your garage. And I hope you do it all somewhere far away from here."

Then the office door opened in.

I guess you already knew that Cassandra was sitting

there. Wearing really high-end corporate gear from Italian designers who had managed to stay out of the international backlash against the American export market. Cortez Enterprises was about to have its limited public offering, I learned later, using a brokerage subsidiary that they owned themselves. So they had tarted up the office to impress some analysts. Cassandra was beautiful in a way I probably can't describe, because beauty, ultimately, is outside of language. Though it may have something to do with memory. She was wearing a red bow.

One of Cortez's goons, unless it was Eddie himself, said, "Kevin, I guess you don't really remember your own mother?"

"My mother? What the hell are you talking about?"

Cassandra had cleaned up a lot since I last saw her. Which I was starting to recognize might have been four months ago. It was hard to tell. Still, she was my age, more or less, maybe a few years younger, so how was she supposed to be my mother?

One thing I'll say for Cassandra, she had the kind of compassionate expression a mother should have had. "Are you all right?"

But the goons interfered with this tender moment.

"Okay, shoot 'em up."

"Wait," I said. "I'm already high, I'm already in somebody's memory, I don't even know if it's my own memory anymore, so you're getting me high inside a memory; that's a memory inside a memory, right? When do we come back out to the present, to the part where I'm just a kid trying to make his way?"

"Shut that motherfucker up."

Cassandra volunteered her arm, so I volunteered mine, covered with scars now, so much that they couldn't find a vein.

"Do him in the neck."

So they did. Without asking nicely.

I swirled into the rapture of the deep, far from all the shit that had accumulated since I first started researching the subject of Albertine. You know, my very first memory is of my grandfather, the Chinese immigrant patriarch, after his open-heart surgery. I was maybe three and a half years old. I never believed those memories. I never used to believe memory before an age when a kid could understand *time*. What comes before it? The rapture of the deep is what comes before. Before the scaffolding of time. Memories cartwheeling around in the empty heavens. Anyway, there he was on the stretcher in the living room, where he lived with us, doped on morphine. Doped for a good month, anyway. I can remember the implacable smile on his face: *I'm suffering now, but I came here for you, so you wouldn't have to suffer. So now go and do something. Make my sacrifices into your day at the beach.* It lingered in my consciousness for a moment. From there the howling winds of recollection touched down on my abortive swimming lessons, then a summer on the Cape, walking on the seashore, up through childhood, from one associative leap to the next, all memories with beaches in them, then all memories with singing in them, memories featuring varieties of pie, like this was the very last mainline I was going to have, like they were going to make a biopic about my short life from this footage scrolling through my brain. Everything was roses. I was the smartest kid in my elementary school class, I was the class president. I was a shortstop player. Everything was roses. Until Serena showed up. Serena, who was exactly contemporary with that nameless dread creeping into my daily life. I was the only Asian kid my parents had ever known who panicked; Asians just didn't panic, or they didn't fucking talk about it, man, that was for sure, like that afternoon when I was supposed to take some government-ordered placement exam and I was in the bathroom puking, my father standing outside the door, telling me, in the severest language, that I was a disgrace. What was I going to do, drop out of society? Go work in a dry cleaner's? Recite poetry to the customers while I was doing alterations? Did I think my grandfather had come from Shanghai, et cetera, et cetera, on a boat that almost sank, et cetera, et cetera, so that I could . . . et cetera, et cetera, and then the sound of my mother's voice telling him to lay off, my mother the microbiologist, or epidemiologist, why couldn't I remember my mother's job, she was never home, actually, she was always working. Come on. I called out to the Cortez flunkies, *Hey, you guys, give me another shot, because nothing is chiming, I am telling you there is not a chime left in the belfry.* I was still pressing a wet rag against the wound in my neck when a guy slapped me on the back of the head and told me to shut the fuck up, and then I was again on the Ferris wheel of it all, but I could see my father's tassled loafers, and that's when Jesse Simons was talking to me again, suddenly I was recognizing her voice.

"Kevin, this is the end of the story, where you're going now, because your mother is about to lay her hand on yours, across the desk, Kevin, and that will be the signal that I have to let go. Here's what happens. This next ten minutes of your life enables us to dose the reservoir before Eddie Cortez finds out. We have just eliminated the person who informs on the plot to dose the reservoir, and so we are free to go back in time, by virtue of our collective affection for the city, to augment the water supply. And you know what this means, Kevin, it means that Eddie won't have time to drop the bomb, Kevin. *The bomb.* Because we believe Eddie Cortez drops the bomb, to try to keep us from dosing the reservoir, and he drops it on lower Manhattan because that's where you live in the fall of 2008. We believe that Eddie Cortez, *not* a highly trained sleeper cell of foreign nationals, detonates the uranium bomb, to ensure the dominance of Cortez Enterprises and to wipe out a number of key Resistance players living in the East Village at that historical juncture. So take your time in the next few minutes, because this gives us the element of surprise we need. Jean-Pierre Al-Sadir is driving a minivan up what's left of the interstate. And I believe he's playing Duke Ellington on the CD player because he wants to hear something really great before his memory is wiped clean. You're the hero of the story, Kevin. And we're all really sorry we couldn't tell you earlier, and we're sorry you had to learn this way. But we want you to know this. We want you to know that all the traumatic events of the last few months, these were things we knew you could withstand. Like few others. You're the kid who made the story for us. We're proud. We wish you were our son. And in a way you are now. If that's any help at all. When you get to Manhattan, after talking to your mother, if it's still *gone*, that'll be the sign. Manhattan in ruins. Your ferry driver will be wearing green. That'll mean that Eddie doesn't need to go back in time to try to find you. That'll mean that

Eddie has given up trying to control the past in order to control the present. Well, unless by poisoning the reservoir we eliminate the future in which Eddie *comes up with the idea* of detonating the blast, in which case Manhattan will still be standing and this entire present, with the drug epidemic and the Brooklyn Resistance, will be nonactualizing. And it's also possible that *the forgetting* will have set in somewhere along the line, we aren't sure where yet, and that you may have forgotten certain important parts of the story. You may have forgotten that Manhattan was ever a city by the time you get home tonight. You might have forgotten all of this, all this rotten stuff, this loneliness, even this speech I'm giving you now. In fact, we have tried to pinpoint forgetting, Kevin; we have targeted it in such a way as to wipe clean your own memories of the blast. Because you actually had a pretty rotten time that day. You saw some awful things. So if you have forgotten, we believe you are the first locally targeted forgetter. However, if in the future, during this forgetting, you want to remember this or other events from your life, we have a suggestion for the future, Kevin: *just play back your audio recordings.*"

This is where my mom stole into my memory of the past. My mom was so beautiful. Every time I saw her. Even when she was Cassandra, on the swing in Brooklyn. So beautiful that I couldn't even see the lines of time carved into her. Here in memory she's young again, she's perfect, young and brilliant, lit in the color of a fading silver halide print. My mom looks Kodak to me, always will, and she leads me out of the bathroom, away from my dad, and she explains that Serena telephoned her, and her syllables are carefully measured like on a metronome. It's not nearly as bad as it seems.

If I could redo the color balance in this past, I would make it more ultramarine, because everything's too yellow, my mother taking me into the living room, where my grandfather once slept off his open-heart surgery. She sits me down. And she makes her diagnosis. She says, *I have been doing a lot of research into your chemical problem. And I have talked to a lot of professional friends on the subject. When you have a spare hour or so, later in the week, then we're going in to talk to some of them. But in the meantime, I want you to try something for me.*

So here it was. In a stoppered beaker.

Just give this a try. I think it'll be more interesting than that stuff you and your friends have been smoking.

Mom, I said. *Do you think I should?*

I'm your mom.

What is it?

Lithium, some SSRIs, and a memory enhancer we're trying out, in an aspartame sauce. It's supposed to sharpen cognition. Might help with those tests.

Just like in the laboratory sequences, you know, from those black-and-white movies of yore. I drank up. And the thing was, I aced that exam. That's what I had forgotten. And I gave some to Serena, and she gave it to her boyfriend, Paley. We called it Albertine because it sounded like aspartame. Or so I was remembering. I gave it to the others. We all did well on our tests. Just three kids from the subdivisions fucking up the entire future of the human race, in pursuit of kicks and decent board scores.

I didn't want to open my eyes. I didn't want to know. Didn't want to look across the desk at Cassandra, who may or may not have been my mother, may or may not have been the chief chemist for the Cortez syndicate, may or may not have been an informer for the Resistance, may or may not have been a young woman, may or may not have been home in Newton, refusing to come to the phone, may or may not have been an older Chinese woman with those sad eyes. I didn't want to hear her voice, from across the room, rationalizing, "Let time show why I've done what I've done." I didn't want to know. I didn't want to know the plans the Cortez operatives had for me, Addict Zero, didn't want to know why I was being put through this exercise—so that they could break me on the rack of information, or because they still wanted me to write down whatever it was that they wanted me to write down. I didn't want to know, finally, which memory was inside of which memory, didn't want to know if there was a truth on top of these other truths. In a few minutes' time, the water supply would be boiling with the stuff, *eight weeks back.* The cops at the reservoirs would be facedown in pools of blood, and the taps in Brooklyn, Queens, Staten Island, and the Bronx would be running bluer than usual, and there would be dancing in the streets, as though all this stuff I'm telling you hadn't happened at all. I mean, assuming the sweet forgetting didn't come like the instantaneous wave of radiation after the blast. Assuming I didn't *forget* all of this, how I got where I got, what I'd once known, the order in which I knew it, the cast of characters, my own name, the denouement.

What's memory? Memory's the groove. It's the all-stars laying down their groove, and it's you dancing, chasing the desperations of the heart, chasing something that's so gone, so ephemeral you know it only by its traces, how a certain plucked guitar string summons the thundering centuries, how a taste of fresh cherries calls up the indolent romancers on antebellum porches, all these stories of the past rolling around in you. Memory is the groove, the lie, the story you never get right, the better place. Memory is the bitch, the shame factory, the curse, and the consolation. And that's where my journalistic exposé breaks down.

But I can offer a few last tidbits. If you're wondering what the future looks like, if you're one of the citizens from the past, wondering, let me tell you what it's like. First thing I'll tell you, gentle reader, is that the Brooklyn Bridge is *gone*, probably the most beautiful structure ever built according to the madness of New Yorkers. Brooklyn Bridge is gone, or at least the half of it on the New York side is gone. The section on the Brooklyn side goes out as far as the first set of pillars, and after that it just crumbles away. Like the arms of Venus de Milo. It's a suggestion of an idealized relationship between parts of a city, a suggestion, not an actual relationship. And maybe that's why intrepid lovers go there now, lovers with thyroid cancer go up there at night, because it's finally a time in New York City history when you can see the night sky. That is, if the wind's blowing toward Jersey. They go up there, the lovers, they jump the police barriers, they walk out on that boardwalk, the part that's still remaining, they look across the East River, they make their protestations of loyalty, *I don't really have much time, so there's a few things I want to say to you.* I'll go even further. Because this instant is endless for me, and that's why I'm dictating these notes. What I do is, I find the ferryman on the Brooklyn side, out in Bay Ridge, old Irish guy, I pay my fresh coin to the Irish ferryman with the green windbreaker, pet his rottweiler. I say, *I got some business over there,* and the guy says, *No can do, pal,* and I point at it and I say, *Business*, and he says, *No one has business there*, but I do, I tell him, and I will make it worth your while, and he says, *There's nothing over there*, but in the end he accepts the offer, and then we are out upon the water, where the currents are stiff and the waves treacherous, as if nature wants to wash this experiment of a city out into the sea, as if nature wants to clean the wound, flush the leftover uranium, the rubble, the human particulate. We're on the water, and right there is where the statue used to be, we'll get the new one from France before too long, and that's where New York Plaza used to be on the tip there. I tell the ferryman to take me farther up the coast; I want to know every rock and piling, every remaining I beam, I want to know it all, so we go past the footprint of South Street Seaport, and here are the things that we lost that I might have seen from here: the Municipal Building with its spires, City Hall, the World Financial Center, the New York Stock Exchange— where did all those bond traders go, what are they doing now, are they in Montclair or Greenwich?—and then it's Chinatown, bombed almost to China, bombed down to the bedrock, edged by Canal Street, which is again a canal, as it was way back when, and Little Italy is gone, those mobster hangouts are all gone, they're all working on the Jersey side now, trying to corner the Albertine market there, and Soho is gone, the former CBGB, New York University is gone, Zeckendorf Towers gone, Union Square Park is gone, the building where Andy Warhol's factory once was, what used to be Max's Kansas City, and the Empire State Building is gone, which, when it fell *sideways*, crushed a huge chunk of lower Fifth Avenue, all the way to the Flatiron District, the area formerly known as the Ladies Mile; the flower district is gone, the Fashion Institute of Technology; in fact, about the only thing they say is still somewhat intact, like the Acropolis in Athens, is the public library, but I can't see it from here. The bridges are blown out, the tram at Fifty-ninth Street gone, and as we pull alongside a section of the island where I'm guessing Stuyvesant Village used to be, I say, *Ferryman, put me down here*, pull your rowboat with its two-horsepower lawn mower engine alongside, because *I'm going in*, I'm going down to Tompkins Square, man, I'm going backward, through that neighborhood of immigrants. So now I step on the easternmost part of the island, same place the Italians stepped, same place the Irish stepped, same place the Puerto Ricans stepped, and I'm going in there now, because as long as it's rubble I don't care how hot it is, I'm going in, it's like a desert of glass, landfill burned into glass, and I can hear the voices, even though it's been a while now, all those voices layered over one another, in their hundred and fifty languages, can't hear anything distinct about what they are saying, except that they are saying, *Hey, time for us to be heard*.

Acknowledgments

Thanks to Dave Eggers and Michael Chabon, whose assignment to write a genre story resulted in "The Albertine Notes." "The Omega Force" was similarly written at the behest of Brigid Hughes, Elizabeth Gaffney, and Fiona Maazel, and in memory of George Plimpton, who is missed by one and all. "K&K," like several other things I have composed, is Amy Hempel's fault. Thanks also to Michael, Pat, the Heathers, and everyone else at Little, Brown; to Melanie and Anne at the Melanie Jackson Agency; to my parents; to my brother and to the rest of my family, especially my nieces and nephews, Ross, Anna, Dylan, Caitlyn, and Tyler.

About the Author

Rick Moody is the author of four novels, two prior collections of stories, and a memoir, *The Black Veil*, for which he received the PEN/Martha Albrand Award. He is also the recipient of the Addison Metcalf Award from the American Academy of Arts and Letters, the *Paris Review*'s Aga Khan Prize, and a Guggenheim Fellowship. He lives with his wife, Amy Osborn, in Brooklyn, New York.